ACCLAIM FOR DAVID MALOUF'S

Dream Stuff

"At an advanced point in his already prolific career, the Australian writer David Malouf has produced a book of fresh beginnings . . . his prose is as tightly under control as his poetry."
—*The New York Review of Books*

"With writing as revelatory as it is eerily precise, that disturbs as much as it satisfies: one and all these masterful stories are such stuff as dreams are made of." —*Kirkus Reviews*

"A beguiling introduction to the work of a writer whose refusal to offer easy answers will wake serious readers from their reveries and keep them thinking for many nights to come."
—*New York* magazine

"Packed with vivid description." —*Book World*

"[Malouf] shows a rare, exploratory intelligence coupled with a compassionate view of human conduct." —*Publishers Weekly*

DAVID MALOUF

Dream Stuff

David Malouf is the author of ten novels and six
volumes of poetry. His novel *The Great World* was
awarded both the prestigious Commonwealth Prize
and the Prix Fémina étranger. *Remembering Babylon*
was short-listed for the Booker Prize. David Malouf
was named the Neustadt Laureat for 2000. He lives
in Sydney, Australia.

INTERNATIONAL

Dream Stuff

Dream Stuff

STORIES

☯

DAVID MALOUF

Vintage International

VINTAGE BOOKS

A DIVISION OF RANDOM HOUSE, INC.

NEW YORK

FIRST VINTAGE INTERNATIONAL EDITION, DECEMBER 2001

Some of the stories were originally published as follows: "Closer" in
Granta; "Night Training" in the *Sydney Morning Herald Good Weekend
Magazine*; "Jacko's Reach" in *A Sea Change*, edited by Adam Shoemaker.

The Library of Congress has cataloged the Pantheon edition as follows:
Malouf, David, 1934–
Dream stuff: stories / David Malouf.
p. cm.
Contents: At Schindler's—Closer—Dream stuff—Night training—Sally's
story—Jacko's reach—Lone pine—Blacksoil country—Great day.
ISBN 0-375-42053-3
I. Australia—Social life and customs—Fiction. I. Title.
PR9619.3.M265 D74 2000 823—dc21 99-088859

Vintage ISBN: 0-375-72449-4

www.vintagebooks.com

Printed in the United States of America
10 9 8 7 6 5 4 3 2 1

Contents

©©

At Schindler's : 1

Closer : 25

Dream Stuff : 33

Night Training : 64

Sally's Story : 74

Jacko's Reach : 93

Lone Pine : 101

Blacksoil Country : 116

Great Day : 131

Dream Stuff

At Schindler's

❦

I

AT Schindler's Jack woke early. The sound of the sea would find its way into his sleep. The little waves of the bay, washing in and receding, dragging the shell-grit after them, would hush his body to their rhythm and carry him back to shallows where he was rolled in salt. It was his own sweat springing warm where the sun struck the glass of his sleepout, which was so much hotter than the rest of the house that he might, in sleep, have drifted twenty degrees north into the tropics where the war was: to Borneo, Malaya, Thailand. He would throw off even the top sheet then to bake in it, till it was too hot, too hot altogether, and he would get up, go down barefoot to pee in a damp place under one of the banana trees and take a bit of a walk round the garden. Until Dolfie, the youngest of the Schindlers, came out bad-tempered and sleepy-eyed to chop wood, he had the garden's long half-acre to himself.

There was a pool at Schindler's. In the old days Jack and his father had swum there each morning. Jack would cling to the edge and kick, while his father, high up on the matted board, would leap, jackknife in the air, hang a moment as if he had miraculously discovered the gift of flight, then plummet and disappear. Then, just when Jack thought he was gone altogether, there would be a splash and he would reappear, head streaming, a performance that gave Jack, after the long wait in which his own breath too was held, a shock of delighted surprise that never lost its appeal.

Schindler's was a boarding house down the 'Bay' at Scarborough. They went there every holidays.

The pool these days was empty, closed, like so much else, for the 'duration'. But Jack, who this year would have been old enough to use the board, liked each morning to walk out to the end and test its spring. Toes curled, arms raised, beautifully balanced between the two blues, the cloudless blue of the early-morning sky and the painted one that was its ideal reflection, he would reach for what he remembered of his father's stance up there, grip the edge, strain skywards with his fingertips, push his ribcage out till the skin felt paper-thin, and hang there, poised.

He had got this part of it perfect. For the rest he would have to be patient and wait.

HIS father was missing – that was the official definition. Or, more hopefully, he was a prisoner of war. More hopefully because wars have a foreseeable end, their prisoners come home: to be missing is to have stepped into a cloud. Jack's mother, who was aware of this, never let a mealtime pass without in some way evoking him.

'I suppose,' she would say, 'your daddy will be having a bite to eat about now.'

They knew quite well he wouldn't be sitting down, as they were, to chops and boiled pudding, but it kept him, even if all he was doing was pushing a few spoonfuls of sticky rice into his mouth, alive and in the same moment with them.

When St Patrick's Day came round she would say: 'Sweet peas. They're your father's favourites. You should remember that, Jack. Maybe by the time they're ready he will be home.'

One year, struck by one of the models in a Paton and Baldwin pattern book, she knitted a cable-stitch sweater for him. Jack held the wool when it was wound, watching the yards and yards it would take pass over his hands. Twenty skeins! When all the parts were finished and had been assembled into the shape of a sweater, his mother held it up to her shoulders. 'Look, Jack.'

He was astonished by the bulkiness of it. He hadn't remembered his father's being so big. In a moment when his mother was out of the room he held its roughness to his cheek, but all he could smell was new wool.

Collapsed now between layers of tissue, it lay in a drawer of his father's lowboy acquiring an odour of naphthalene.

But as the months slipped by and they still had no news of him, no postcard or message on the radio, Jack saw that his mother's assurance had begun to fail. She still spoke as if his father were just out of the room for a bit, at a football match or having a drink down at the boat club, but she was pretending. For his sake – that is what he felt – and it worried him that she might realize that he knew. They would have to admit something then, and it was imperative, he thought, that they should not. If she no longer had faith, then he must. If his father was to survive and get home, if he was to hang on to whatever light thread was keeping him in the world, then *he* was the one who must keep believing. It was up to him.

* * *

'Now, Milly! You can't just sit around mooning. Stan wouldn't want that. You're young, you need a break. You need to get out and have a bit of fun.'

This was his Aunt Susan speaking, his father's sister. Jack wondered how she could do it.

'Look,' she said, holding his mother's hair up, 'like this. You've got such lovely bones.'

They looked into the mirror, his aunt lifting the thick hair in her hands like a live animal, their two bodies leaning close.

His mother regarded herself. 'Do you really think so?' she said dreamily. 'That I could get away with it?'

Jack frowned. Don't, Mum, he said silently.

The two figures in the mirror, his mother smiling now, her head turned to one side, disturbed him; there was a kind of complicity between them. When they looked at one another and leaned closer, their eyes full of daring and barely suppressed hilarity, he felt they had moved away into a place where he was not invited to follow. Other rules applied there than the ones he knew and wanted her to keep.

'Well, I don't know,' his mother was saying. But she looked pleased, and his Aunt Susan giggled. 'Maybe,' she said. 'What do you think, Jack?'

He looked away and did not answer. She must know as well as he did that his father hated anything of that sort – rouge, painted toenails, permed hair. What was wrong with her?

For the past few weeks she had been working one night a week at a canteen. Now, under his Aunt Susan's influence, she changed her hairstyle to a glossy pompadour, put on wedgies and, drawing Jack into it as well, began to teach herself the newest dances. They tried them out with old gramophone records, on the back verandah; Jack rather awkward in bare feet and very aware that he came only to her shoulder. I'm only doing it to make her happy, he told himself. He felt none of the pride and excitement of the previous year, when he had gone along each Saturday night in a white shirt and bow tie to be her beau at the Scarborough dances.

Americans began to appear at their door. Escorts, they were called. It had a military ring, more formal, less personal than partner. They brought his mother orchids in a square cellophane box and, for him, 'candy', which only Americans could get. He accepted, it was only polite, but made it clear that he had not been bought.

His mother asked him what he thought of these escorts and they laughed together over their various failings. She was more critical than Jack himself might have been and this pleased him. She also consulted him about what she should wear, and would change if he disapproved. He was not deceived by any of this, but did not let her see it.

And in fact no harm was done. New dances replaced the old ones every month or so, and in the same way the Rudis, the Dukes, the Vergils, the Kents, were around for a bit and sat tugging at their collars under the tasselled lamps while his mother, out in the kitchen, fixed her corsage and they made half-hearted attempts to interest or impress him, then one after another they got their marching orders. Within a week or two of making themselves too easily at home, putting their boots up on the coffee-table, swigging beer from the bottle, they were gone. The war took them. They moved on.

MILT, Milton J. Schuster the Third, was an Air Force navigator from Hartford, Connecticut, a lanky, fair-headed fellow, younger than the others, with an adam's apple that jumped about when he was excited and glasses of a kind Jack had never seen before, just lenses without frames. Jack took to him immediately.

He wasn't a loud-mouth like so many of the others, he did not skite. And for all that he was so young, he had done a lot, and was full of odd bits of information and facts that were new to Jack and endlessly interesting. But most of all, it was Milt who was new. He was put together with so much lazy energy, had so many skills, so much experience that he was ready, in his good-humoured way, to share.

'Jack,' his mother protested, 'give us a break, will you? That's the fifty-seventh question you've asked since tea.'

But where Milt was concerned Jack could never get to the end of his whats and whys and how comes and who said sos, or of Milt's teasing and sometimes crazy answers.

Milt was a fixer. Humming to himself a tuneless tune that you could never quite catch, comfortable in a sweat-stained singlet with the dog-tags hanging, he would, without looking up from the screwdriver he was spinning in his long fingers or the fuse-wire he was unravelling, say 'Hi, kiddo,' the same for Jack and his mother both, and just go on being absorbed. It wasn't an invitation to stay, but it wasn't a hint either (Jack was sensitive to these) that you should push off. He accepted your presence and went on being alone. Yet somehow you were not left out.

In fact the jobs Milt did were things Jack's mother could do quite well herself, but she was happy now to have Milt do them. When he made a lamp come on that had, for goodness knows how long, failed to work, he wore such a look of beaming satisfaction that he might have supplied the power for it out of his own abundant nature, out of the same energy that fired his long stride and lit his smile.

So what was his secret? That's what Jack wanted to know. That was where all his questions tended. And what was the tune he hummed? It seemed to Jack that if he could only get close enough to hear it, he would understand at last Milt's peculiar magic. Because it was magic of a sort. It put a spell on you. Only

Milt didn't seem to know that he possessed it, and it was this not-knowing, Jack thought, that made it so mysterious, but also made it work.

Milt was twenty-two. In the strict code of those times it was inconceivable that a woman should be interested in a man who was younger. Jack could imagine his mother breaking some of the rules, smoking in the street for instance, or whistling, but not this one. So he had come to think of Milt as *his* friend.

When Christmas came they took him to Schindler's.

II

THEY had been going to Schindler's for as long as Jack could remember. His mother and father had spent their honeymoon there. Unlike the other guests, who ate in the little sunlit dining-room at midday and half-past six, they took their meals at the big table in Mrs Schindler's kitchen, and Jack had permission to go in at any hour and ask for milk from the fridge, or an ice-block, or one of Mrs Schindler's homemade biscuits. On days when they went fishing at Deception, Mary, the Schindler's girl, packed them a lunch-tin with things only the family ate: salami, sweet-and-sour gherkins, strudel.

The soil at Scarborough was red. So were the eroded cliffs, which you could slide down and whose granular, packed earth could be trickled through a fist to colour sand-gardens. So were the rocks that formed a Point at each end of the beach, and the escarpments of the reef that at low tide emerged from the dazzle about sixty yards out, where fishermen, standing on the streaming shelf, cast lines for rock-cod or bream.

When the tide was in the Points were covered, the beach was isolated. But at low tide, walking on what had just an hour before been the bottom of the sea, you could go round by the beach way to Redcliffe in one direction or Deception in the other.

No need to consult the *Courier Mail* for high- and low-water times at the Pile Light. When the tide was coming in your sandfly bites grew swollen and itched. When it went out, they stopped.

The beach at Scarborough was a family camping-ground. Bounded on one side by a grassy cliff-top – where at Christmas there was a fairground with hoopla stalls and an Octopus and a woozy merry-go-round – and on the other by a storm-water drain, it was a city of tents; or if not a city, at least a good-sized township, where the same groups, established in the same pozzies each year, made up a community as fixed in its way as any on the map.

It was a lively and relaxed world. When the tent-flaps were up people's whole lives were visible, the folding table where they ate, the galvanized or enamel tub where they washed their clothes and did the dishes, the primus stove, camp-stretchers and carbide or petrol lamps. Jack spent his whole day moving from tent to tent asking if his friends could come out, or being gathered into the loose arrangements that were other people's lives. There were a dozen families where he could simply step in under the flap, which would be golden where the sun beat through, and be offered a slice of bread with condensed milk or, in the afternoon, a chunk of cold watermelon.

At home in Brisbane, people's lives were out of sight behind lattice and venetians. Here, it was as if, in some holiday version of themselves, they had nothing to hide. All you had to do to be one of them was to make yourself visible; and if, in tribute to settled convention, you did say 'knock, knock', it was a kind of joke, the merest shadowy acknowledgment of the existence elsewhere of doors and of a privacy that had already been surrendered or was dissolved here like the walls.

'Come on in, pet.' That is what Mrs Chester or Mrs Williams would call, the comfortable mothers of his holiday friends. And if strangers were there, other women like themselves, barefoot, in beltless frocks, they might add: 'This is Jack. He's one of the family, aren't you, love?'

It was a manner of speaking, a temporary truth like all their arrangements down here. Rivalries, gangs, friendships existed with a passionate intensity for the six weeks of Christmas and two more at Easter, and for the rest of the year, like some of the rivers they drew in Geography, went underground, became dotted lines.

Jack loved these broken continuities. They were reassuring. You let things drop out of sight, then you picked them up again further on. Nothing was lost. Even a single day could have that pattern. For a whole morning, while you played Fish or Ludo, you were one of the Chesters. Then in the afternoon you became a loose adjunct of the Ludlow family or returned to your own.

It was his own family that was the puzzle.

The way Jack saw it was this. He and his mother were two points of a triangle, of which the third point was over the horizon somewhere in a place he could conceive of but never reach, though there were times when his whole body ached towards it, and so intensely that he would wake at night with the torment of it. Growing pains, his mother called it. And it was true, he was growing; he had shot up suddenly into a beanpole. But that wasn't the whole of it.

Down here at Scarborough, where he was most keenly aware of his body as the immediate image of himself, the sun's heat, day after day, and especially in the early morning when it struck the glass of his hot-house sleepout, would draw him in a half-waking dream to some tropic place where everything grew faster. His limbs would be stretched then across three thousand miles of real space till every joint was racked, and he would experience at last the thing he most hungered for: a smell of roll-your-owns as sharp as if his father were actually there in the room with him, or a light-headed feeling of being hefted all along the verandah-boards on his father's boot, the two of them laughing, Jack a little out of fear, and his father shouting: 'Hang on, Jack, that's the boy. Hang on!'

It was the voice he found hardest to keep hold of. He strained to hear it, vigorously lifted, under the beating of the shower, 'All together for the Floral Dance', but got nowhere. When he did sometimes discern the peculiar line of it on a stranger's lips it was in one of the phrases his father liked to use: 'fair crack o' the whip' or 'you wouldn' credit it.' He would try for the tune of it then under his breath.

So here they were at Schindler's; Jack, his mother, and Milt. Jack was in his element.

Even Mrs Schindler, who had treated Milt at first with a kind of coldness, was won over by the drawling stories he told, a way he had of kidding people that was rough but inviting. By the end of their first meal together she adored him and from then on insisted on making all his favourite dishes, waiting breathlessly, like a girl, for him to taste and approve. Once it had been Jack who was consulted on whether the precious dessert-spoons should be used for ice-cream or for pudding. Now it was Milt. And Jack didn't mind at all. How could he be resentful of someone he himself was so eager to see pleased?

Milt kidded Mrs Schindler the way he kidded Jack's mother, with a mixture of courtliness and plain tomfoolery. He hung around the kitchen benches, beating eggs and dipping his finger into bowls. He set up a little speaker so that Mrs Schindler could listen in to the news from the lounge-room wireless while she helped Mary wash up. He danced her all round the kitchen, on the black and white tiles, whistling 'Wiener Blut'.

Jack still spent the day with his friends down at the beach, but in the evenings he and Milt played Chinese Checkers or Fiddlesticks, or the three of them played Euchre, or Milt worked with him on the crystal set he was making while his mother read. They went fishing at Deception, roller-skating at Redcliffe, and some afternoons he and Milt went off alone to the Redcliffe Pictures. Milt was crazy about cartoons. He sat with his long legs drawn up, cracking peanuts, and afterwards acted it all out again for Jack's mother – Bugs Bunny, Tom and Jerry, Goofy, Pluto – running about all over the room being a rabbit, a tom-cat, a mouse, and reducing her to helpless laughter as she never would have been by the real thing. Once, walking home the beach way, he told Jack about the fossils he wanted to study: palaeontology – bones. He got excited, threw his own bones about, arms and legs, and Jack had to run backwards on his heels over the wet sand not to miss any of it, since so much of what Milt was telling was in the dance of his adam's apple, the electric spikes of his crew-cut hair.

'How do you do it?' Jack shouted, excited himself now and breathless with trying to run backwards fast enough to stay in front. 'How do you work it out? What they were like? If they've been extinct for millions of years? If all you've got is a few bones?'

'Logic,' Milt told him, looking wild. 'There are laws. We don't get this way by accident, you know. We aren't just thrown together.' Though the way his limbs were flying about, as if they were about to dislocate and break loose of his frame, might have denied it. 'The body's got laws, and the bones follow 'em, just like everything else. It's a kind of – grammar – syntax. You know, everything fits and agrees. So if you've got one bit you can work out the rest, you can – resurrect it. By logic. But also by guessing right. There's a lot of guesswork involved, hunches. You've got to think yourself inside the thing, into the bones.'

It had all gone too fast for Jack. Running backwards wasn't the ideal way to hear something so important and take it in. But he felt, just the same, that in this shouted exchange he had got hold at last of an important clue, one that convinced him because, in some obscure part of himself, he already knew it. When they fell into step again, saying nothing now, just letting the fall of the waves fill the silence between them, they were together, and in a way that utterly settled him in his own skin.

I T was a happy time for Jack's mother too.

A lively girl with ideas of her own, she had been brought up to despise a view of women in which dependency and a sweet incapacity for everything practical were the chief attributes of the eternally feminine.

'For heaven's sake,' she was fond of saying, 'what's the advantage, I'd like to know, of sitting around in the dark until some *man* comes along who can fix a fuse.'

She knew how to fix a fuse, and use a soldering iron, and how to bowl overarm and putt a ball. She had done these things when Jack's father was there, and when he was gone had taught Jack to do them, but with some concern that in having only her to learn from he might be missing something, some male thing, beyond the mere acquiring of a competence, that would ground him in the world of men. So she was glad to have Milt around. Glad too that Jack had taken to him. He had a new sense of himself that she found attractive – she had found it attractive in his father, whom he more and more resembled – and she was grateful that Milt, out of a natural generosity, should have reserved for Jack something that was special. It was part of Milt's instinct for things that he knew how to draw back and leave room for something special between Jack and herself as well.

'No good asking you to play,' she would tease when they set up for cricket. And her mocking tone, which Milt only pretended not to recognize, kept him lightly in view, even as it lightly excluded him.

It was a tone Jack had never heard her use till now. And once he was alerted to it, he noticed something else as well. A little shift in her way of speaking – it was only on certain words – that was an imitation, a mockery perhaps, of Milt's. It occurred to him, but so fleetingly that he was barely conscious of it, that if he could determine which words, he would have a clue to what they talked about, Milt and his mother, when he was not there.

Meanwhile Milt's replies, all Yankee ceremony, had an edge of their own.

'No use at all, ma'am. None at all.' And as he said it he would lie back, extend his long legs and, with his arms folded under his head, prepare to take a nap.

He was grinning, so was Jack's mother, and Jack had the feeling that their game of two-man cricket was not the only game in play. When his mother got hold of the bat she hit out with a flair, a keenness and accuracy, that had him running all over the yard.

In time he came to feel uncomfortable with all this. There was something in his mother's heightened glow on these occasions, when Milt lay sprawling in the grass, a loose spectator, not playing but none the less exerting a quiet attraction, that was more disturbing to Jack's fixed idea of her than other and more obvious changes – the ribbon she wore in her hair when they went skating, her acceptance now and then of a stick of gum.

He had a good think about it.

Milt, he decided, lying off to the side there, broke the clear line of force between batsman and bowler. His mother was too aware of him. Even more, he unsettled the map Jack carried in his head, in which the third point of their triangle, however far out of sight it might be, was already occupied.

They would be out on the pier at Deception, all three, their handlines trailing, stunned to a heap by the sun and with the glare off the water so strong that when you looked out across it everything dazzled and disappeared. Above the lapping, against the piles, of waves set off by a distant rowboat, Jack would catch a voice he could no longer characterize naming the peaks of the Glasshouse Mountains on the opposite shore: Coochin, Beerwah, Beerburrum, Ngungun, Coonowrin, Tibrogargan, Tiberoowuccum. Smokily invisible today in their dance over the plain, but nameable, even in a tongue in which they were no more than evocative syllables.

'Hey, kid! Jack! Don't jerk the line like that. Take it easy, eh?'

That was Milt. And his voice, with its unmistakable cadence, was sufficiently unlike the one Jack had been listening for that it was a comfort. It so plainly did not fit.

III

AMONG Jack's special friends this year were two brothers, Gerald and Jamie Garrett, who were new down here. Tough State School kids, they swore, told dirty jokes and could produce prodigious gobs of spit that they shot like bullets from between their teeth. But what gave them a special glamour in Jack's eyes was their father's occupation. Back home in Brisbane, Mr Garrett was the projectionist at the Lyric Pictures where Jack went on Saturday afternoons, and was responsible as well for putting up the posters that appeared in three places on Jack's way to school and which on Monday mornings he read, right down to the smallest print, with an excitement that cast a glow over the whole week ahead.

What they proclaimed, these posters, was the existence of another world, of such modernity, such intensified energy and speed, of danger too, that their local one of weatherboard houses and bakers' carts, unweeded pavements and trams that filled the night sky with electric sparks, seemed by comparison flimsy and becalmed. America, that world was called. It moved on numbered highways at a hundred miles an hour. It was twenty storeys high, all steel and glass. It belonged to a century that for them was still to come. Jack hungered for it, and for the dramas that it would unfold, as for his own manhood.

He had looked for some reflection of all this in his mother's escorts. But once you had got to the end of whatever magic could be extracted from 'Santa Fe' or 'Wisconsin' or 'Arkansas', they had turned out to be ordinary fellows off farms, or small-town car salesmen or pharmacists' assistants. As for Milt, he was just Milt. But in Mr Garrett the power of that projected world was primary, and he found it undiminished in Gerald and Jamie as well, who would have been astonished to know that in Jack's eyes they were touched with all the menacing distinction of the gun-slinger or baby-faced killer.

There was a third brother. Arnold he was called. A year older than Jack, he was spending the first three weeks of the holidays at their grandfather's, out west. Gerald and Jamie, as if they needed his being there to know quite how they stood with one another and the world, were forever evoking his opinion or using his approval or disapproval to justify their own. Before long the tantalizing absence of this middle brother had become a vital aspect of the Garretts as Jack saw them, and he too found himself looking forward to Arnold's arrival. 'Arnold'll be here next week, eh?' Then it was 'Saturday'. Then 'this arvo'.

But Arnold, when he got off the green bus and was there at last, was not at all what Jack had expected. The quality he found in the others, of menace and tough allure, far from being intensified in this third member of the family, appeared to have missed him altogether. Blond where the others were dark, and tanned and freckled, he seemed dreamy, distant. When they told him stories of what had been, for them, the high points of these last weeks, he listened, but in the way, Jack thought, that adults listen to kids. Not disdainfully, he was too easygoing to be disdainful, but as if he could no longer quite recall what it was like to be involved in adventures or crazes. When he left school next year he would be out west permanently. On the land.

His most prized possessions were a pair of scuffed riding boots that sat side by side under his camp-bed and a belt of plaited kangaroo hide that cinched in the waist of his shorts with a good seven or eight inches to spare. He had ridden buckjumpers. He could skin a rabbit.

He did not boast of these things. He was not the sort to draw attention to himself or be loud. But the assurance they gave him, the adult skills they represented, set in a different light the excitements that had marked their weeks down here; even the abandoned fuel tank that had drifted in one afternoon and which they had believed, for a long, breathtaking moment while it bobbed about just out of reach, might be a midget sub.

'Anyway,' Arnold assured them, 'them Japs wouldn' get far, even if they did land. Not out there.' And he evoked such horizons when he lifted his eyes in the following silence that the walk to Redcliffe or Deception, even the bush way, seemed like nothing.

Arnold Garrett had the slowest, drawliest voice Jack had ever heard. Secretly, high up on the diving-board or in the privacy of his room, he would reach for the growling flatness of it, 'Aout theere,' in the belief that if he could get the tone right he might catch a glimpse, through the other boy's eyes, of what it was.

There were times, listening to Arnold and narrowing his eyes in the same heat-struck gaze, when Jack felt turned about. Away from the Bay and its red rocks, away from their gangs, their games, this particular school holidays and everything to do with being eleven, or twelve even, towards—

But there he came to a barrier that Arnold Garrett, he felt, had already crossed.

THEY were sitting around after a late-afternoon swim. Jack was in the middle of a story, one of those flights of fancy with which he could sometimes hold them, all attention, in a tight group, when Arnold said lightly: 'Hey, are you a Yank or something? You talk like a Yank,' and he repeated a phrase Jack had used, with such dead accuracy, such perfect mimicry of Jack's pitch and tone and the decidedly un-local accent he had given to the otherwise innocent word 'water', that the whole group, Gerald, Jamie, the Williams boys, laughed outright. Jack was dumbstruck. It wasn't simply that it was, of all people, Arnold who had caught him out in this small defection from the local, but the thing itself. He flushed with shame.

'It's his mum,' Jamie explained. 'She goes out with one.' He said this in a matter-of-fact way. There was a touch of scorn but no malice in it.

'She does not,' Jack shouted, and even as he flung the insinuation back at them he saw that it was true.

'Doesn't she?' Jamie said. 'It's what Dolfie Schindler said. What about—'

But Jack, his face burning, had already leapt to his feet. Filled with the crazy conviction that if he denied it with his whole body it would cease to be true, he struck out, though not at Jamie. Honour would not allow him to strike a younger boy.

'Hey,' Arnold yelled, throwing him off. 'Hey! Are you crazy or something? Lay off!' Then, seeing that Jack could not be stopped, he weighed in with his fists and they fought, all knuckles, elbows and knees, tumbling over one another on the coarse seagrass and pigface in a flurry of sand. When it was over they were both bloodied, but neither had won. 'You're crazy,' Jamie shouted after him as he strode away.

He was still shaking. Not only with the passion of the fight and the hard blows he had taken, but with the shock of what he had discovered, which the furious involvement of blood and limbs and sweat and breath had failed to mitigate or change. He went and sat under the pump where the campers came to fetch water, tugging on the bit of looped wire that worked the handle and letting gush after gush of chill water pummel his skull. He sat with his arms around his drawn-up knees, uncontrollably shaking, and the tears he shed were hidden by the rush of water, and the din it made replaced for a moment the turbulence of his thoughts.

'Looks like you picked the wrong guy,' Milt remarked when he came in. One cheek was raw and he had the beginnings of a black eye.

'Jack!' his mother exclaimed. 'This isn't like you.'

He couldn't look at either of them and shrugged his shoulders when they asked if he was all right.

They treated him gently after that. Warily. Trying not to make too much of it. As if, he thought, they preferred not to know why he had been fighting, or not to have it said. It was Mrs Schindler who tended his cheek. But when she tried to cuddle him, he slipped out of her grip, and when Dolfie, at the end of their meal, waited as usual for him to help carry scraps out to the chooks, he turned his back on him. 'You can drop dead,' he hissed. His only comfort was his wounds.

A T either end of the beach at Scarborough was a twelve-foot-high slippery-slide, a tower of raw saplings with a ladder on one side, its rungs so widely spaced that you had to be nine or ten years old to climb them, and on the other a polished chute. On the platform between, four or five kids could huddle, waiting their turn and threatening to shove one another off, or sit with their legs dangling while sunlight crusted the salt on their backs.

For a long time Jack had been too young for the slippery-slide. Then, last Christmas, when he was ready, he had been shocked to discover that he had no head for heights. The climb was all right; so was the slide. The bad bit was having to wait on the platform. In his dream he found himself alone up there with a king tide running.

He was in deep trouble. Dark water rushed and foamed out of sight below, the flimsy structure shuddered and creaked. Worse still, the saplings that supported the platform had done their own growing in his sleep, so that when he shuffled forward on his knees to look over the edge, his head reeled. How had he found the courage to climb so high, to make his arms reach across the space between the rungs? No wonder his whole body ached. In the end there was nothing for it but to jump himself awake. It was the only way down.

He was sweating. Silvery flashes lashed the louvres of the sleepout. They rattled in their frames. The tin roof drummed. They got these storms along the coast down here, in January when the king tides were running.

He rolled out of bed.

Barefoot, in just his pyjama bottoms and still shaken by his dream, he stepped outside and, like a child younger than his present self, a six-year-old still scared of the dark, started off down the verandah to where his parents slept.

Rain was beating in under the rails, forming pools of lightning round every post. Rivulets followed the cracks in the floorboards. Careful not to get his feet wet, he stepped over them – he was awake enough for that – and turned the corner towards his mother's room, which was halfway down the long side of the house, facing the front.

When he came to the french doors, they were open. The rain on the roof was deafening.

His first thought was that he had found his way back to a time, three years ago, when his father was still here. There were two figures on the bed.

Or – his mind worked slowly – or his mother had hit upon a way of summoning his father to her in the night. Some spell. His heart leapt. Daddy! Dad! The words were already on his lips.

The two figures were fiercely engaged. He knew what it was, what they were doing. He had heard the facts of it. But nothing he had been told or imagined was a preparation for the extent to which, in their utter absorption in one another, they had freed themselves of all restraint. They were at a point of concentrated savagery that for all its intensity of thrusting and clutching was not violent, not at all, and not scary either, though it did set his heart beating.

His mother's head was thrown back and flinging from side to side. Her mouth was open, moaning. And Milt's breadth of shoulders and long back – for it was Milt, he could see that now – was rising and falling to the tune she sang, or it was Milt's tune they moved to, and she had discovered it, the one he hummed under his breath. What Jack was reminded of was moments when, in a kind of freedom that only his body had access to, he ceased for a time to be a boy and became a porpoise, rolling over and under the skin of sunlight all down the length of the Bay. Under the waves, then over. Entering, emerging. From air to water, then back again.

There was a lightning flash. The whole room for a moment was blindingly illuminated, the high ceiling, the walls, the rippled sheet and the figures beneath it. And there, on the other side of the bed, glimpsed only for the merest second before it fell back into the half-dark, was another figure, also watching.

It was his father. Bare-ribbed, long-necked, in a pair of old pyjama bottoms that hung below the hollow of his belly, he stood watching, in an exclusion that made him ghostlike, as if the world he belonged to was the otherworld of the dead. Jack strained to make him out there, to hold on to the sight of him. And realized, with a little shock, what the apparition really was. Not a ghost, but himself, fantastically elongated in the glass of the old-fashioned wardrobe.

Something snapped then. He heard it. A sound louder than the crack of thunder or the rising climax of their cries, or his own smaller one, which they were too far off now in the far place to which their bodies had carried them to hear.

HE stood, barefoot and still in pyjamas, at the very edge of the diving-board above the empty pool, using his weight to test the springs. He did not raise his arms or practise his pose.

The garden had been badly hit. There were smashed branches all over, and the pool had leaves in it and puddles where tiny frogs squatted and leapt. There was a strangeness. Some of it was in the light. But some of it, he knew, was in him. Keeping as close as possible to his normal routine, he went in, changed into a pair of shorts, and went out through the gate, across the road and down the red-soil track to the beach.

It was early, just before six, but men were already out tightening guy-ropes, digging new trenches round their camps. There was a high tide running. It was grey, its dull waves crested with weed as if a gigantic shark out there were showing first its back, then its belly, leaden, dangerous. Little kids, standing on isolated hillocks in the dunes, were gesturing towards it, marvelling at the absence of beach, dancing about on a ledge of soft sand that fell abruptly to foam.

He went on to the north end where the storm-water channel ran all the way to the water's edge, in a tangle of yellow-flowering native hibiscus so dense and anciently intertwined that without once setting your foot to the ground you could move on through it all the way to the beach. He swung up on to a low branch and made his way along it, gripping with his toes and using his arms for balance, then hauled himself on to a new branch higher up.

It was another world up here, a place so hidden and old, so deeply mythologized by the games they played in the twists and turns of its branches, their invented world of tribes and wars and castles, that the moment you hauled yourself up into its big-leafed light and shade you shook loose of the actual, were freed of ground rules and the habits of a life lived on floorboards and in rooms.

Hauling himself up from branch to branch, higher than he had ever been before, he found a place where he was invisible from below but had the whole Bay before him.

It was an established custom that they came to the Trees only in the afternoon. He had the place to himself. Feeling the damp air begin to heat, he settled and let himself sink into an easy state where it was his blood that did the thinking for him, or his thumbs, or the small of his back where it was set hard against rough bark. From high up among leaves he watched the tide turn and begin, imperceptibly at first, then with swiftness, to go out.

His father would not be coming back. That was the first fact he had to face. And the second was that his mother already knew and had accepted it. Somewhere too deep for thought, he too had known it. The pain and bafflement of his first reaction had been at some failure of his own: he had let his father go; his will had not been strong enough to prevent him from slipping away. But he saw now that that was foolish. There were things that were out of your control. And if this was scary, it was also a relief. There were happenings out there in the world that you were not responsible for.

He must have slept then, because when he looked out again the morning had moved on. The sun was out. Mothers were pegging clothes to improvised lines, along with towels and old rags that had been used to sop up the rain. Others were dragging out furniture as well, stretcher-beds and mattresses, suitcases, the wooden, gauze-sided cupboards where groceries were kept. Fathers were going from tent to tent inspecting damage, tendering advice. He could see it all from up here. Weak rays were lighting the tent-flaps and the tarpaulins laid out on the grass, but would soon be stronger.

Inside, card games would be starting up, Fish or Grab for the littlies, Euchre for the older kids, or Pontoon or Poker. He did not have to look in to see any of this.

Fran Williams would be laid across a stretcher with *The Count of Monte Cristo* open on the grass below. The Ludlow girls would have set up their grocery shop, its cardboard shelves stacked with tiny packets of tea, rice, sugar, sago, and little stamped coins in piles to shop with. Along the shoreline, processions of treasure-hunters were poking about among the rubble of seaweed and cuttlefish shells and Have-a-Heart sticks.

Eventually, not long from now, he would go down and join them, and later again, not too late, not too early either, but at his usual hour, he would make his way back to Schindler's.

He sat a little longer, enjoying the sense that there was no rush. In a state of easy well-being. Refreshed, restored. Then, as slowly as he had come, he began to make his way back down through the open tangle; at one moment poised upright, at another crouched and reaching out till he could find a further branch to swing on, then hanging, then swinging out again in the slowest sort of flying twenty feet above the ground.

If he had bothered to think about it he would have said that he was happy. But as he came to the last of the trees and dropped lightly to the sand, he was thinking only that he was hungry and could do with a bit of breakfast and how hot the sun felt on his shoulders and how good it would be to put his hand out, have Arnold Garrett take it, and know that all was well again.

Not entirely well. There was a shadow on his heart that would be there for many years to come, a feeling of loss from which he would only slowly be released. But he was too young to conceive of more years than he had known, and the sun was getting hotter by the minute, and a little kid he had seen often enough but had never spoken to was hailing him from the top of a dune. 'Hey,' he called, 'is your name Jack? There's some boys been lookin' for you, all over. I know where they are if you like. Hey,' he said, 'what about that? They been lookin' all over and I'm the one that found you.'

No you didn't, he might have told him, I wasn't lost. But the boy was so pleased with himself that Jack did not want to disappoint him. 'Come on,' he said, and they set off together down the ravaged beach.

Closer

❧❧

THERE was a time, not so long ago, when we saw my Uncle Charles twice each year, at Easter and Christmas. He lives in Sydney but would come like the rest of us to eat at the big table at my grandmother's, after church. We're Pentecostals. We believe that all that is written in the Book is clear truth without error. Just as it is written, so it is. Some of us speak in tongues and others have the gift of laying on hands. This is a grace we are granted because we live as the Lord wishes, in truth and charity.

My name is Amy, but in the family I am called Ay, and my brothers, Mark and Ben, call me Rabbit. Next year, when I am ten, and can think for myself and resist the influences, I will go to school like the boys. In the meantime my grandmother teaches me. I am past long division.

Uncle Charles is the eldest son, the firstborn. When you see him in family photographs with my mother and Uncle James and Uncle Matt, he is the blondest; his eyes have the most sparkle to them. My mother says he was always the rebel. She says his trouble is he never grew up. He lives in Sydney, which Grandpa Morpeth says is Sodom. This is the literal truth, as Aaron's rod, which he threw at Pharaoh's feet, did literally become a serpent and Jesus turned water into wine. The Lord destroyed Sodom and he is destroying Sydney, but with fire this time that is slow and invisible. It is burning people up but you don't see it because they burn from within. That's at the beginning. Later, they burn visibly, and the sight of the flames blistering and scorching and blackening and wasting to the bone is horrible.

Because Uncle Charles lives in Sodom we do not let him visit. If we did, we might be touched. He is one of the fools in Israel — that is what Grandpa Morpeth calls him. He has practised abominations. Three years ago he confessed this to my Grandpa and Grandma and my Uncle James and Matt, expecting them to welcome his frankness. Since then he is banished, he is as water spilled on the ground that cannot be gathered up again. So that we will not be infected by the plague he carries, Grandpa has forbidden him to come on to the land. In fact, he is forbidden to come at all, though he does come, at Easter and Christmas, when we see him across the home-paddock fence. He stands far back on the other side and my grandfather and grandmother and the rest of us stand on ours, on the grass slope below the house.

We live in separate houses but on the same farm, which is where my mother and Uncle James and Uncle Matt, and Uncle Charles when he was young, grew up, and where my Uncles James and Matt still work.

They are big men with hands swollen and scabbed from the farm work they do, and burnt necks and faces, and feet with toenails grey from sloshing about in rubber boots in the bails. They barge about the kitchen at five o'clock in their undershorts, still half asleep, then sit waiting for Grandma to butter their toast and pour their tea. Then they go out and milk the herd, hose out the bails, drive the cows to pasture and cut and stack lucerne for winter feed – sometimes my brothers and I go with them. They are blond like Uncle Charles, but not so blond, and the hair that climbs out above their singlets, under the adam's apple, is dark. They are jokers, they like to fool about. They are always teasing. They have a wild streak but have learned to keep it in. My mother says they should marry and have wives.

Working a dairy farm is a healthy life. The work is hard but good. But when I grow up I mean to be an astronaut.

Ours is a very pleasant part of the country. We are blessed. The cattle are fat, the pasture's good. The older farmhouses, like my grandfather's, are large, with many rooms and wide verandahs, surrounded by camphor-laurels, and bunyas and hoop-pines and Scotch firs. Sodom is far off, but one of the stations on the line is at the bottom of our hill and many trains go back and forth. My Uncle Charles, however, comes by car.

His car is silver. It is a BMW and cost an arm and a leg. It has sheepskin seat covers and a hands-free phone. When Uncle Charles is on the way he likes to call and announce his progress.

The telephone rings in the hallway. You answer. There are pips, then Uncle Charles says in a jokey kind of voice: 'This is GAY 437 calling. I am approaching Bulahdelah.' The air roaring through the car makes his voice sound weird, like a spaceman's. Far off. It is like a spaceship homing in.

Later he calls again. 'This is GAY 437,' the voice announces. 'I am approaching Wauchope.'

'Don't any one of you pick up that phone,' my grandfather orders.

'But, Grandpa,' my brother Ben says, 'it might be Mrs McTaggart.' Mrs McTaggart is a widow and our neighbour.

'It won't be,' Grandpa says. 'It will be him.'

He is a stranger to us, as if he had never been born. This is what Grandpa says. My grandmother says nothing. She was in labour for thirty-two hours with Uncle Charles, he was her first. For her, it can never be as if he had never been born, even if she too has cast him out. I heard my mother say this. My father told her to shush.

You can see his car coming from far off. You can see it *approaching*. It is very like a spaceship, silver and fast; it flashes. You can see its windscreen catching the sun as it rounds the curves between the big Norfolk Island pines of the golf course and the hospital, then its flash flash between the trees along the river. When it pulls up on the road outside our gate there is a humming like something from another world, then all four windows go up of their own accord, all together, with no one winding, and Uncle Charles swings the driver's door open and steps out.

He is taller than Uncle James or Uncle Matt, taller even than Grandpa, and has what the Book calls beautiful locks. They are blond. 'Bleached,' my grandfather tells us. 'Peroxide!' He is tanned and has the whitest teeth I have ever seen.

The corruption is invisible. The fire is under his clothes and inside him, hidden beneath the tan.

The dogs arrive, yelping. All bunched together, they go bounding over the grass to the fence, leaping up on one another's backs with their tails wagging to lick his hands as he reaches in to fondle them.

'Don't come any closer,' my grandfather shouts. 'We can see you from there.'

His voice is gruff, as if he had suddenly caught cold, which in fact he never does, or as if a stranger was speaking for him. Uncle Charles has broken his heart. Grandpa has cast him out, as you cut off a limb so that the body can go on living. But he likes to see that he is still okay. That it has not yet begun.

And in fact he looks wonderful – as far as you can see. No marks.

Once when he got out of the car he had his shirt off. His chest had scoops of shadow and his shoulders were golden and so smooth they gave off a glow. His whole body had a sheen to it.

Uncle James and Uncle Matt are hairy men like Esau, they are shaggy. But his chest and throat and arms were like an angel's, smooth and polished as wood.

You see the whiteness of his teeth, and when he takes off his sunglasses the sparkle of his eyes, and his smoothness and the blondness of his hair, but you do not see the marks. This is because he does not come close.

My grandmother stands with her hands clasped, and breathes but does not speak. Neither does my mother, though I have heard her say to my father, in an argument: 'Charlie's just a big kid. He never grew up. He was always such fun to be with.'

'Helen!' my father said.

I know my grandmother would like Uncle Charles to come closer so that she could really see how he looks. She would like him to come in and eat. There is always enough, we are blessed. There is an ivory ring with his initial on it, C, in the dresser drawer with the napkins, and when we count the places at table she pretends to make a mistake, out of habit, and sets one extra. But not the ring. The place stays empty all through our meal. No one mentions it.

I know it is Grandpa Morpeth's heart that is broken, because he has said so, but it is Grandma Morpeth who feels it most. She likes to touch. She is always lifting you up and hugging. She does not talk much.

When we go in to eat and take up our napkins and say grace and begin passing things, he does not leave; he stays there beside his car in the burning sunlight. Sometimes he walks up and down outside the fence and shouts. It is hot. You can feel the burning sweat on him. Then, after a time, he stops shouting and there is silence. Then the door of his car slams and he roars off.

I would get up if I was allowed and watch the flash flash of metal as he takes the curves round the river, past the hospital, then the golf course. But by the time everyone is finished and we are allowed to get down, he is gone. There is just the wide green pasture, open and empty, with clouds making giant shadows and the trees by the river in a silvery shimmer, all their leaves humming a little and twinkling as they turn over in a breeze that otherwise you might not have felt.

Evil is in the world because of men and their tendency to sin. Men fell into error so there is sin, and because of sin there is death. Once the error has got in, there is no fixing it. Not in this world. But it is sad, that, it is hard. Grandpa says it has to be; that we must do what is hard to show that we love what is good and hate what is sinful, and the harder the thing, the more love we show Him.

But I don't understand about love any more than I do about death. It seems harder than anyone can bear to stand on one side of the fence and have Uncle Charles stand there on the other. As if he was already dead, and death was stronger than love, which surely cannot be.

When we sit down to our meal, with his chair an empty space, the food we eat has no savour. I watch Grandpa Morpeth cut pieces of meat with his big hands and push them between his teeth, and chew and swallow, and what he is eating, I know, is ashes. His heart is closed on its grief. And that is what love is. That is what death is. Us inside at the table, passing things and eating, and him outside, as if he had never been born; dead to us, but shouting. The silver car with its dusky windows that roll up of their own accord and the phone in there in its cradle is the chariot of death, and the voice announcing, 'I am on the way, I am approaching Gloucester, I am approaching Taree' – what can that be but the angel of death?

The phone rings in the house. It rings and rings. We pause at the sink, in the middle of washing up, my grandmother and my mother and me, but do not look at one another. My grandfather says: 'Don't touch it. Let it ring.' So it keeps ringing for a while, then stops. Like the shouting.

This Easter for the first time he did not come. We waited for the telephone to ring and I went out, just before we sat down to our meal, to look for the flash of his car along the river. Nothing. Just the wide green landscape lying still under the heat, with not a sign of movement in it.

That night I had a dream, and in the dream he did come. We stood below the verandah and watched his car pull up outside the fence. The smoky windows went up, as usual. But when the door swung open and he got out, it was not just his shirt he had taken off, but all his clothes, even his shoes and socks. Everything except his sunglasses. You could see his bare feet in the grass, large and bony, and he glowed, he was smooth all over, like an angel.

He began to walk up to the fence. When he came to it he stood still a moment, frowning. Then he put his hand out and walked on, walked right through it to our side, where we were waiting. What I thought, in the dream, was that the lumpy coarse-stemmed grass was the same on both sides, so why not? If one thick blade didn't know any more than another that the fence was there, why should his feet?

When he saw what he had done he stopped, looked back at the fence and laughed. All around his feet, little daisies and gaudy, bright pink clover flowers began to appear, and the petals glowed like metal, molten in the sun but cool, and spread uphill to where we were standing, and were soon all around us and under our shoes. Insects, tiny grasshoppers, sprang up and went leaping, and glassy snails no bigger than your little fingernail hung on the grass stems, quietly feeding. He took off his sunglasses, looked down at them and laughed. Then looked across to where we were, waiting. I had such a feeling of lightness and happiness it was as if my bones had been changed into clouds, just as the tough grass had been changed into flowers.

I knew it was a dream. But dreams can be messages. The feeling that comes with them is real, and if you hold on to it you can make the rest real. So I thought: if he can't come to us, I must go to him.

So this is what I do. I picture him. There on the other side of the fence, naked, his feet pressing the springy grass. *Stretch out your hand*, I tell him. *Like this*. I stretch my hand out. *If you have faith, the fence will open for you, as the sea did before Moses when he reached out his hand*. He looks puzzled. *No*, I tell him, *don't think about it. Just let it happen*.

It has not happened yet. But it will. Then, when he is close at last, when he has passed through the fence and is on our side, I will stretch out my hand and touch him, just under the left breast, and he will be whole. He will feel it happening to him and laugh. His laughter will be the proof. I want this more than anything. It is my heart's desire.

Each night now I lie quiet in the dark and go over it. The winding up of the smoky windows of the chariot of death. The swinging open of the door. Him stepping out and looking towards me behind his sunglasses. Me telling him what I tell myself:

Open your heart now. Let it happen. Come closer, closer. See? Now reach out your hand.

Dream Stuff

◎◎

I

COLIN'S earliest memory was of the day his mother's doberman Maxie died, of heartworm, they said; he had dragged himself up under the house near the front steps and would not come out.

Late in the morning Colin slipped away and, crawling on his hands and knees in the dirt, though the place had always scared him – it was all dustballs and spiders, some of them just shells but others alive and skittering – he had gone up after Maxie and crouched there holding the big floppy creature in his arms.

The slats that closed in their under-the-house made the place dim, even in daylight. But up where Maxie lay, still drawing breath, there was the fleshy green light of the gladioli stems that rose stiffly on either side of their front steps.

Colin stayed up there the whole day, hugging Maxie and listening to footsteps in the rooms overhead: Mrs Hull going from room to room as she swept and made beds, then coming heavy-footed down the hallway to the postman, then going out the back again for the ice.

About lunchtime they began calling to him. Casually at first, then with increasing anxiety. Mrs Hull, then his mother, then, joining them, the first of the ladies who had arrived for Bridge. Finally – it was afternoon by now – his father, who had been called home from work.

'Colin,' his father said severely from far off where their wash-tubs stood, 'come on out of there.'

But he turned his face away and would not be persuaded.

His father, handing his jacket to Mr Hull, started up through the forest of stumps, crouched at first, then crawling, then wriggling on his belly. His tie was loose, his cufflinks jingled. Colin could hear them and the heavy breathing as his father emerged from the middle darkness and came up to where there was light.

'Colin,' he said, 'what are you doing? Come on out, son. It's time to come out.'

'No,' he said. 'Not unless Maxie does.'

'Colin, Maxie is very sick, we can't help him. Now, be a good fellow and come out.' The voice was exasperated but calm, holding on hard against shortness of breath rather than shortness of temper.

Colin had no memory of what happened next. The story as they told it simply trailed off, or led, in that anthology of anecdote and legend that is family history, to another story altogether. The occasion remained suspended at a point where he was still crammed into the close space under the floorboards, with the big dog warm in his arms and the whole weight of the house on his shoulders, while his father, dark-faced and wheezy with hay-fever, stretched a hand towards him, all the fingers tense to grasp or be grasped, and his brow greasy with sweat; as if he were the one who was trapped up there dying – the worm at his heart taking all his breath.

This image was overlaid with another from perhaps a year later.

They were staying at his grandfather's house at Woody Point. His father was teaching him to swim. One afternoon, after several attempts to make him let go and strike out for himself, his father carried him out of his depth in the still, salty water and, breaking contact, stepped away. 'Now, Colin,' he commanded, 'swim'.

His father's face, just feet away, was grim and unyielding. He floundered, flinging his arms about wildly, gasping, his throat tight with the saltiness that was both the ocean and his own tears. He dared not open his mouth to cry out. He choked, while his father, his features those of a stony god, continued to urge him and back away.

As Colin saw himself, he wore, as he gasped and thrashed at the surface, the same look of desperation that he had seen in his father when, with his chin thrust up and the muscles of his neck horribly distended as his whole body fought for breath, he lay stretched on his belly in the dust.

So it was from somewhere far up under their house at Red Hill, or choking in the waters off Woody Point, that he woke now to his hotel bedroom and a climate established somewhere in an unearthly season between autumn and early spring, in a place that might have been anywhere but was in fact, for the first time in nearly thirty years, home – that is, the city he had grown up in, though when he went to the window there was little that recalled that exotic and far-off place save a lingering warmth out of his dream and a tightening of anxiety in his throat.

All that belonged to the interior view. Down below, in the real one, the big country town of his childhood, with its wharves and bond-stores and two-storey verandahed pubs, had been levelled to make way for flyovers, multi-level carparks, tower blocks that flashed like tinfoil and warped what they reflected – which was steel girders, other towers like themselves and cranes that swung like giant insects from cloud to cloud. Brisbane, as his cousin Coralie put it, had 'gone ahead'. It was a phrase people used here with a mixture of uneasy pride and barbed, protective humour, expecting him, out of affection for the slatternly, poor-white city of his youth, to deplore this new addiction to metal and glass.

Well, he did and he did not. It wasn't nostalgia for a world that had long since disappeared under fathoms of poured concrete that had led him, in half a dozen fictions, to raise it again in the density of tropical vegetation, timber soft to the thumb, the drumming of rain on corrugated-iron roofs. What drew him back was something altogether more personal, which belonged to the body and its hot affinities, to a history where, in the pain and longing of adolescence, he was still standing at the corner of Queen and Albert Streets waiting for someone he knew now would never appear.

He had long understood that one of his selves, the earliest and most vulnerable, had never left this place, and that his original and clearest view of things could be recovered only through what had first come to him in the glow of its ordinary light and weather. In a fig tree taller than a building and alive with voices not its own, or a line of palings with a gap you could crawl through into a wilderness of nut-grass and cosmos and saw-legged grasshoppers as big as wrens.

It was the light they appeared in that was the point, and that at least had not changed. It fell on the new city with the same promise of an ordinary grace as on the old. He greeted it with the delight of recovery, not only of the vision but of himself.

HE had left the place when he was not yet twenty. That was the year his mother went back to Sydney.

Twenty-three years earlier, his father, on a weekend rowing trip, had discovered her there and brought her north. She had never really settled. When she put the old house up for auction and went home, Colin had seized the chance to make his own escape. He went to London. Till now he had not come back.

In the twenty years that they lived together he had found his mother a puzzle, and where his need for affection was concerned, a frustration.

A lean ghost of a woman, intense, but not in his way, she had prowled the house with an ashtray in her hand, distractedly chain-smoking, argued with friends on the phone, mostly men-friends, gone to committee meetings and charity drives, and was always interested, out of a sense of duty, in his doings but reticent about her own. Dissatisfied, he thought, maybe desperate – he could not tell, and he knew she would not have wanted him to ask. She made no enquiry about *his* feelings. They got through his childhood and adolescence without ever being close.

Then something unexpected occurred. Freed by distance, they found a way of being intimate at last. Perhaps it was the writing itself that did it. Anyway, the letters she sent him, warm, inventive, humorously critical of everything she came across (he recognized, he thought, and with curiosity now, the tone of her telephone conversations), were those of a woman he more and more wanted to know. So much of what he was haunted by, all that underworld of his early memories and their crooked history, was in her keeping. If he was ever to get to the heart of it he would need her as his guide.

He no longer tormented himself with the wish that things had been different. They had made him what he was. But he did want to know why the world he had grown up in had been so harsh and uncompromising, and had made so little room for love.

Then there was the question of his father. His father had disappeared in the waters off Crete in May 1942. Swimming out on a night of no moon to be rescued along with other remnants of a defeated army by the British submarine *Torbay*, he had tired and gone under.

Colin, who was just six, had believed for a time that he was actually there and had seen it happen, but understood at last that he had been imposing on that moonless night on the far side of the world the only clear memories he had of his father and their time together; though even then there was part of him in which his presence out there, in those dark unknown waters, remained more vivid than either.

Each year as Christmas drew near he would suggest to his mother that he should come and visit. They would see one another at last and talk.

How wonderful, she wrote. How she would look forward to it. But she managed, each time, to find excuses, and he guessed that she was unwilling to put to the test this long-distance intimacy that had grown up between them. Her dying suddenly, with no suggestion of a previous illness, made him wonder how much more she had been keeping from him.

Arriving before the last of his letters, he put it into the coffin along with the many other questions to which he must accept now that there would be no answer, and since he was here, and un-likely to come back a second time, accepted an invitation to fly up to Brisbane and give a reading.

It was a strange homecoming. He knew no one in Brisbane but his cousin Corrie. He was forty-eight years old and nobody's child.

ONE of the few mementoes his father had left was a little green-bound pocket diary in which, for a few days in Athens, in the year of his death, he had recorded in his Queenslander's big copybook hand what he had seen of a city whose every monument he had already wandered through in dreams, but which had to be excavated, by the time he got there, from towers of rubble.

What moved Colin when he first turned its pages was the passion he found even in the driest details, and the glimpse he got, which was clear but fleeting, of a young man he felt close to but had barely known, and who had himself to be resurrected now from scribbled notes and statistics, tiny painstaking sketches of capitals and the motifs off daggers in a dusty museum, and from half a dozen hastily scrawled street maps.

He stuffed the diary into the bottom of his rucksack and when, at the end of his first year in Europe, he went to Athens, spent a whole day trying to match the sketches to a modern map of the city.

What he had hoped to recover was some defining image of his father, some more intimate view of the amateur classicist and champion athlete who had played so large and yet so ghostly a part in his existence. He stood at corner after corner turning the sketch-map this way and that until, admitting at last that he was bushed, he took himself off to a café on Venizelou.

He was settled there in front of a cold beer, still sweating, when he was approached by a dandified stranger, a fellow not much older, he guessed, than himself, but with a gold wedding-band on his finger, who seemed to have mistaken him for someone else. Anyway, they got talking, and when his new friend, out of pure pride in the place, offered to show him around a little – the sights, the real sights – he accepted.

His guide was so knowledgeable, he talked so well and in such impeccable English, that Colin, who had been wary at first, was soon at his ease. And it was astonishing how often it happened that Giorgios in his excitable way said: 'Look, Colin, now look at this,' and there it was, just what the diary had described as being wonderful but hard to come upon and which on his own he had been unable to find.

They moved deeper and deeper into a maze. After the classical sights, the Byzantine – though 'after' in fact was not quite accurate, because everything here was a patchwork in which bits of one period were used to hold up or decorate another, a half-column here, a slab there with two peacocks and a laurel wreath, so that styles and centuries tended to collapse into one another. As the afternoon wore on, the sights closed in. They were in a tangle of narrow streets where men with baskets were selling twists of salt-crusted bread and sticky honey-cakes; a crowded place, noisy, garish, where his new friend seemed to know everyone they met, and introduced him to men who showed him brasswork and filigree silver and other antique relics, but gave out, in an obscure way, that they had other wares to dispose of, though he could not guess what they might be and his new friend did not elucidate.

They stepped into one dark little taverna to drink ouzo, and into another to smoke, and afterwards he had the sensation that time, as he had already discovered among the monuments, was more a continual looping here than a straight line. He half expected, as a narrow street turned back upon itself, to see his father appear in the shadowy crowd, though there was no indication in the diary that he had been in this place. Then quite suddenly, in a poky alleyway with stalls full of brazen pots and icons, his friend was gone.

It was the oddest thing imaginable. One minute he was there, as affable and eager as ever, and the next he had slipped away.

There was no misunderstanding. Or if there was, Colin had

failed to observe it. Perhaps his guide had lost patience with him, with his failure — was that it? — to catch at suggestions. Or he had seen friends close by and, not wishing to desert him openly — anyway, the occasion was broken off, that is what Colin felt. Things had been moving towards some event or revelation that at the last moment, for whatever reason, had been withheld.

He was disappointed for a time, but came at last to feel that it might have been the best thing after all. He heard tales later of tourists, too trusting like himself, who had been led on and then robbed or assaulted. Perhaps the fellow had thought better of it and let him off. But the teasing suggestion of something more to come, which was unseen but strongly felt, and had to be puzzled over and guessed at, appealed to him. To a side of him that preferred not to come to conclusions. That lived most richly in mystery and suspended expectation. The afternoon had a shape that he came to feel was exemplary, and his readers might have been surprised to know how often the fictions he created derived their vagrant form, but even more their mixture of openness and hidden, half-sought-for menace, from an occasion he had never got to the bottom of, for all that he had gone back time after time and let his imagination play with its many possibilities.

So now, shaved, showered and with a pot of strong coffee at his elbow, he got down to it, the usual routine.

He wrote quickly, his blood brightening the moment he took up where he had left off the day before. His people drew breath again, turned their mute, expectant faces towards him.

He had moved the desk so that it faced the wall. The sun was already high and the city in a swelter, but the room he was writing in seemed within reach of invisible snow peaks. He wrote in coolness, while down there in weatherboard houses under weeping figs, behind mango and banana trees and spindly rust-coloured palms, his people sweated it out; till just on four in the afternoon, as a longish paragraph found its way towards that hour, the sky cracked, struck, and a storm broke, turning closed rooms into gigantic side-drums crazily beaten and shutting off, for a time, all chance of speech.

He put his pen down. It was almost ten. Quite soon his hosts would appear. That cloudburst had cleared the air. He could leave his people suspended in it, waiting to hear how they should go on.

It had cleared his own head as well, giving things, when he went to the window, an intense glow as if lit from within. The big trees in the Gardens opposite, that in their darkness of packed leaves might have been sinister, seemed filled with a powerful energy: gigantic angels momentarily stilled.

Greenness, that was the thing. Irresistible growth. Though it wasn't always an image of health or of fullness.

He thought of the mangroves with their roots in mud, and under their misshapen arches the stick-eyes of crabs and their ponderous claws. They had been banished for a time under concrete freeways, but would soon be pushing up fleshy roots, their leathery leaves, black rather than green, agleam with salt.

Vegetation spread quickly here. Everything spread quickly – germs, butter, rumours. There was talk of plantations outside the city, in pockets deep in the foothills of the Range, where cannabis was being grown in dense plantations. Each night late, trucks would move into the city, on the lookout for teenagers who had nowhere to sleep or were simply loose in the streets, available for whatever might bring a little action into their lives. They would be approached, hired, loaded on to trucks, and driven blindfold to the marijuana fields, where in long rows, until first light, they would go about the business of harvesting the green stuff, the dream stuff. Then, towards four-thirty, when the sun began to show, after being paid and blindfolded again, they would be driven back and dropped off in the Valley or at Stones Corner, or along the various bus routes into the city.

True? It did not have to be. It was convincing at some deeper level than fact. It expressed something that was continuous with the underground history of the place, with triangles and flayed ribs, the leper colony on its island in the Bay, the men with scabbed and bloody hands sleeping on sacks behind the Markets, an emanation in heavy light and in green, subaqueous air, of an aboriginal misery that no tower block or flyover could entirely obliterate.

He moved one of his characters into place somewhere along Petrie Terrace where he could be approached. Loose, open, waiting for the truck that had just set out from a covered shed and was wobbling, low down on a rutted track, under moonlit leaves.

It was ten. Precisely. Any moment now his cousin Corrie would ring.

II

HE and Coralie had grown up together. In the war years, with his father gone and his mother taken up with a social round that had a new definition as war work, he had spent the long weeks of the Christmas holidays at his Grandfather Lattimer's house at Woody Point, in a muddle of uncles and aunts and their children of whom Coralie James, who was just his age, had always been closest to him. In the obsessive way of only children they had done everything in tandem, having discovered in one another feelings they had thought too private, too much their own and only theirs, to be shared. They exchanged whispered secrets, scared one another with ghost stories, had their own coded language full of private jokes and references, which they would recognize only later as another version of the Lattimer exclusivity, and had, at eight or nine years old, to the amusement of the grown-ups, committed themselves to marriage. They had even picked out the house they meant to live in. A two-storeyed cottage with dormer windows, it was sufficiently unlike the houses they and their friends lived in to suggest possibilities of behaviour, of feeling too, quite different from the ones they found unsatisfactory at home.

Well, it had come to nothing, of course. A childish dream. Only once after those early years had he and Coralie spent any time together.

At twenty-five she had turned up in Swinging London, at a time, just after the birth of their second daughter, when he and Jane were still dealing happily with broken nights, babies' bottles, and wet nappies drying on a ceiling rack in the damp little kitchen. Coralie, while she made up her mind between a teaching job in Portugal and a return to the arms of a boy in Brisbane who was prepared to wait, though not perhaps for ever, had spent six weeks on the floor of their basement living-room.

It was the time, as well, of his first novel, which he wrote each night at the kitchen table, in the early hours while his family slept in the room next door; getting up every half-hour or so and stepping away from the warm sunlight of his Brisbane childhood to feed the coke-fire or make himself a mug of tea, and when the baby woke to walk her up and down a little while a bottle heated. His head would be so brimming with sunlight, and images and whole sentences that he needed to set down before they were gone, that he would write on sometimes with the baby over his shoulder, feeding off her warmth, in a state of wholeness and ease with his life and work that he was never to know so completely again.

In the conspiratorial way of lovers, he and Jane had made alliance against their wanted, unwanted guest. When he crept to

bed at last, Jane would tease him about his other woman out there
— and he could never be sure how serious she was and whether it
was Coralie she meant or his book.

And in fact there was a sense in which they could scarcely be
separated, that's what he saw after a time, since it was Coralie's
presence he was drawing on when so many vivid pictures came
back to him. Of blue sand-crabs spilled from a gunnysack and
setting out over the red-earth floor of a hut, till they could be
grabbed by the back legs and dropped squealing into the pot. Of
tiger-moths at a wire-screen door and the peculiar light of a
ribbed sandbank when the tide rippled out and a whole battalion
of soldier crabs wheeled and flashed, then darkened.

'She's still in love with you,' Jane whispered. 'She thinks I'm a
mistake. She thinks I'm the interloper.'

'Don't be silly,' he protested.

'She thinks you two were made for each other. And you love it
— you really love it. Being the rooster with two hens.'

'Do I?' he asked, genuinely surprised but not entirely dis-
pleased with this new and more dashing version of himself.

'Yes, you do — bastard!' Her voice, in playful accusation, had a
throatiness, a sensuality that stirred him. 'At heart you're a
philanderer.'

'No I'm not,' he told her. 'What do you mean? I'm not,' and he
clasped her more warmly in the rumpled bed.

It became a joke between them, one of her ways of playing up
to his ego and exciting him. It had taken him another seven years
to see that it was also true.

But she had been wrong about Coralie. Their moment was
past. He found her presence at the edge of his enclosed and
sufficient family an irritation. Too keen-eyed, too deeply imbued
with their Lattimer scepticism, she was an infidel. He resented her
humorous disbelief in his being so easily settled. Being settled was

important to him – too important, perhaps, that is what she had seen, and if he had been less concerned to defend his own small victory over aimlessness and the fear that without the constraints of a conventional family life he would sink back into the perplexities and self-destructiveness of adolescence, he too might have seen it.

How little he had known himself! What a mess he had made of things. And now, after half a lifetime, this late reunion.

It did not help that Coralie and Jane had remained friends, and that she knew, from Jane's side, all the sorry details, the whole sad story. And would have heard as well that of his two daughters, Eleanor would see him only to make their meetings, each time, the occasion of bitter recriminations and punishment, and Annabel, who had been his favourite, would not see him at all.

They had been to the North Coast – a patchy occasion, despite the perfect weather. Now, sun-dazed, they were having drinks on the Pedersens' verandah above the river. Coralie, shoes discarded, her bare legs tucked away under her, had retreated into silence. It was Eric who did the talking.

All day, intimidated perhaps by the years they had known one another, his wife and this almost famous cousin, and the times they had shared, or by a kind of play between them which was too light, too full of allusions he could not catch, and which represented a side of Corrie he did not feel comfortable with, Eric had been sulky, watchful; determined, Colin thought, not to be drawn in or impressed. Now, suddenly, he had sprung to life. He expanded, he was voluble. It was as if he and Coralie shared a single source of energy, and when one of them drew on it the other wilted. Or perhaps it was simply that he was on home ground at last.

He had just made a surprising discovery. That Colin, who in

all other respects seemed a well-informed sort of chap, was entirely ignorant on the subject of futures.

'I can't believe it,' he kept saying. 'Corrie, can you believe it?'

Futures, it seemed, were what everyone was into.

Eric, in a way that was almost winning, he was so shyly passionate about the thing, began a lecture on futures and how they worked, keeping the tone light – he did not want to appear ponderous – but making certain that Colin should not miss the fact that here too a certain imagination and flair might be demanded. The thing had its own sort of drama, and considering the dreams that were dependent on it, and the suspense and disappointments, might have the makings of a plot.

Colin nodded, but it was like listening to something that, however coherent it might be, made no sense; like a poem in another tongue. Did Coralie follow it? Was she even listening? He could make nothing of the little smile she wore. Anyway, she must have tired of whatever amusement it gave her to see him so easily discomfited. After a moment or two she got up and said: 'Well, I'd better see what I can rustle up to eat.' She was abandoning – no, relinquishing – him. When she called them in, twenty minutes later, Eric had his arm across Colin's shoulder and had become cheerily sentimental. They might have been old friends who had just recaptured, in a series of boyish reminiscences, a moment forty years back when as spirited ten-year-olds they had slit their wrists Indian style and shared blood and spit. Colin did not trust himself to look in Coralie's direction.

'Big things are happening here,' Eric was telling him. 'We're going on by leaps and bounds. No holding us. You ought to come back and be part of it, Colin. We need him, don't we, Corrie?'

'Mango,' Coralie told Colin, who was separating something from the green of his salad, 'and shredded ginger,' and their eyes did meet for a moment. But any alliance between them could only be fleeting. And Eric was too deep in his pleasure in the occasion to see how lightly they let him off. Was she always so indulgent, Colin wondered.

Forgive me, she was saying.

No, he said. No need. I'm the one.

The fact was, he was a disappointment to her. She had read too many of his books. Eric's advantage was that he had read none of them. Then there was Jane, and London, and all those years when they had been so close that he could barely separate, when he looked back, what had been his experience and what hers. He had stolen a good deal of it – she of all people must know how much – and made it his own. But the fact that he had used it in his work did not mean that he had used it up, or got to the end of its mysteries. It was still precious to him, all of it, and she was so much part of the way it played on his mind and on his senses, especially here among so many familiar sounds and objects, that his feeling for her was as fresh and real in him as it had ever been. This is what he had wanted, all day, to say to her. But they had spent the time in small talk. He had said nothing. And in the end it was Eric who had stepped in and claimed him, and would establish the tone of their last hours together.

There was a kind of comedy in that, and they might have to settle for the recognition of it in a shared glance as the nearest they would get, this time round, to their old closeness or the promise of a new one.

'Good night, Colin,' she said softly when the taxi arrived and they went out into the gathered night-sounds of the verandah. The touch of her hand very softly on his cheek was an assurance.

'Good night, mate – keep in touch,' Eric told him, leaning into the window of the taxi. And he called again from the foot of the steps where Coralie fitted into the hollow of his arm: 'And remember, we need you. Come back soon.'

III

THE events of the following hours he would have rejected outright if they had presented themselves to him as the components of a plot. They were too extravagant for the web of quiet incident and subtle shifts of power that were the usual stuff of his fiction. But they occurred and he was not granted the right of refusal. From the moment the Pedersens saw him into the cab (the front seat beside the driver) he was aware that some agency had taken over whose imagination was wilder than his own and which he could neither anticipate nor control.

The driver himself was part of it. Young, bearded, in boxer shorts and sneakers, he was one of the sociable ones, an Armenian or Yugoslav with the broad vowels of the local accent drawlingly prolonged and the consonants of another tongue altogether.

When a few direct questions established that Colin was a visitor, he began evoking possibilities for the remainder of the night: a gambling club, a massage parlour, other darker, more dangerous amenities that were not to be named. When Colin, with a wave of his hand, rejected them, he shrugged and removed himself to a sulky distance, one hairy arm on the steering wheel, the other angled out of the window and drumming lightly on the roof. After five minutes or so of this Colin said abruptly: 'Look, just let me out at the next corner, will you? I need a breath of air. I'll walk.'

The driver pulled in. 'Please yerself,' he said. 'You're the driver.'

He sniggered at his own joke, consulted a card, made calculations, very slowly as if the figures wouldn't add up, and named a price. Safely outside, Colin passed him a note and relinquished the change.

The driver grinned. It wasn't a pleasant grin, and Colin

wondered, as he set off beside a row of dingy shops that appeared sinister but were merely unlit, if the fellow hadn't after all delivered him over to one of those obscure and perhaps hazardous occasions that had not been named.

T H E city at this hour was deserted. The street (and he could see down a dip a good half-mile of it) was clear. He thought of flagging down another cab. But that was silly. He knew this place, he had grown up in it, his hotel was five minutes away, and he had the odd conviction that if he did hail a cab it would turn out to be the one he had just got out of making a circle around the block.

He had gone no more than forty yards – past a gunsmith's, its barred windows stacked with rifles and binoculars, a jeweller's, the frosted windows of a bank – when he was aware of a car, a battered Kingswood, that had slowed to walking pace and was travelling close to the pavement beside him. The driver's head was thrust out, in an effort, he realized, to see him more clearly in the diminished light.

He tried to conceal his anxiety, but began to walk faster. When the Kingswood put on speed at last and swung round the next corner, he crossed briskly against the lights, and was just beginning to regain his composure and admonish himself for being a fool when he heard behind him the footfalls of someone running, and a moment later was being pushed back hard against a wall.

It was a matter of seconds. His attacker, too close for him to get any impression except of damp flesh, had him pinioned and was breathing heat into his neck.

'You din' expect that, didja,' the man hissed. 'Didja? Didja?' With each question he pushed his face closer and jerked Colin's arm. 'You cunt!'

He whispered this almost lovingly into Colin's ear.

'I seen you get outa that car. I knew I'd catch up with you sooner or later. Cunt!'

Colin's panic, now that the situation had declared itself, had given way to raging anger. He was surprised at the intensity of it and at how clear-headed he felt.

'Get off,' he shouted, and raised his elbow and pushed.

'Oh no you don't,' the fellow warned, and he held him even closer, half smiling, very pleased with himself. A lean-faced fellow of maybe thirty, red-headed, unshaven, wearing a singlet. Colin could smell the excitement that came off him, a yeasty sourness. When he was satisfied his grip was firm, he leaned back a little and said easily: 'So here we are, eh? Just the two 'v us.' He gave a short laugh, but seemed now to lose concentration, as if he did not know what should come next. Perhaps his arm was tiring and it had occurred to him that he could not go on holding Colin for ever. 'I seen you get outa that cab,' he said again. Then he found what it was he really wanted to say. 'You din' think I'd face up to yer, didja? Well, you made a bad mistake, feller. I'm fed up t' th' gizzard. I'd rather fucken finish off the both of us.' He said this with passion, his voice rising to a sobbing note, but did not move.

'Look,' Colin said, 'this is crazy. I don't even know who you are.'

'Don't you? Don't you? Well, that's what you would say.'

Once again the energy had gone out of him. He swung his head from side to side as if looking out for something. 'Only I'm not that much of a mug. I know you've been with 'er. I wanta hear you say it. Say it, cunt! Bloody say it!'

These were not so much orders as desperate appeals. When Colin did not respond, the fellow looked about again, and with a forceful motion broke his grip, then stood slumped, his arms hanging. His face was distorted with a pain so naked and hopeless that Colin, who was free now and might have run, was mesmerized. The man raised his voice in a dismal howl. 'Say it,' he sobbed. But hopelessly now, as if the words were a spell that had failed to work, or whose purpose he could no longer recall.

I should get away now, Colin told himself. This is the dangerous bit. That other stuff was nothing. Just bluster. This is it. And almost on the thought a knife appeared in the man's hand. He stepped back, the knife flashed, and with a series of anguished cries he began slashing at the freckled, dead-white flesh of his own neck and shoulder and at the dirty singlet, which was immediately drenched with blood.

'For God's sake!' Colin shouted.

But the man was now triumphant. He stood at the edge of the pavement with his head thrown back in the light of a streetlamp and wielded the knife in slow motion while Colin, helplessly, watched. 'There!' he sobbed, 'There! There!' – as if what he had wanted all along was not Colin's life but his attention, and the sobs came as regular as the gushes of his blood.

Colin, without thinking, made a grab for the knife and felt himself cut.

There was blood everywhere now, some of it on the man's body, some of it on him. The knife slid away into the gutter and they were locked fiercely together on the pavement, grunting and shouting wordlessly between breaths until, with a mechanical whooping and a pulsing of blue light, a car came screaming to a halt beside them and Colin felt himself hauled skywards by a hefty cop. 'Okay, feller,' he was being advised, 'you just calm down, eh?' The incident was at an end.

He was covered with blood. The other man, savagely wounded, was weeping and on his knees.

It wasn't till he was in the squad car, and his heart had slackened a little, that he caught up with the enormity of the thing. The blood that covered his shirt and jacket in a sticky mess was the stranger's. He was barely scratched.

'BUT it doesn't make sense, now does it, Colin?' the larger of the two detectives told him. He was speaking gently, with tolerance for a naïvety that might, after all, be genuine; as one talks to a bemused and stubborn child.

The room seemed too small for the three of them. There was too much light.

'Now, tell us again, Colin. You get out of the cab. Why? What was it that upset you? In what way did this Armenian, or Yugoslav, seem threatening?'

The more often he told it the less probable it became. He saw that. A taxi-driver he had been eager to get away from, at midnight, half a mile from his hotel. A perfect stranger who first attacked and abused him and then turned the knife on himself. The only fact he could produce was his identity.

These sceptical fellows, who had never heard of him of course, were not impressed. 'What sort of books, Colin?' the blond one, who was larger, enquired with a sneer. He was called Lindenmeyer, the other Creager.

After a time they allowed him to ring the Pedersens, and Coralie verified that, yes, he had been with them. They had seen him off in the taxi. The driver was dark. Greek maybe, Lebanese. 'Listen, Colin,' she whispered, when they passed the phone to him, 'don't tell them anything till we get hold of a lawyer. Eric will be there to bail you out. Don't say a word. And most of all, don't provoke them. You don't know what they're like.'

Looking sheepishly at the two detectives, he thanked her. They were grinning. Perfectly aware of what Coralie was telling him, they seemed amused by their own reputation – which did not mean that it was undeserved.

But Coralie was wrong, he did know these men. They were boys he had grown up with, and Lindenmeyer might even have been familiar. It was a name he knew from school.

He was very blond and bony, and must, in early adolescence, have been girlishly pretty. There was, behind his rather high voice and beefy grin, a hint of fineness savagely repressed. Only with women, Colin thought, might he feel free to reveal it. But of the two, it was Lindenmeyer he was wary of. His brutality, like his coarseness, was assumed. Having no necessary cause, it would also have no limit. Creager, more obviously the bully, had no need to make a show. Red Irish and with freckles that in places had turned to open sores, he was all bluster, but too lazy to do more than put a blow in now and then to keep up his name for toughness. It was Lindenmeyer who asked the questions.

So he claimed to be local. Didn't sound it.

And had stepped out of nowhere into a situation with which he had absolutely no connection. Well, he was in the clear then.

Given the state of his clothes and the amount of blood he was covered with, very little of which was his own, and the crusting of it in the cracks of his knuckles and under his nails, there was some justification, he saw, for Lindenmeyer's irony. Blood needs explaining. He recalled, with astonishment now, the sense of elation in which, just before he was hauled off the man, he had been aiming blow after blow at his face.

'Will he be all right?' he found himself asking, and was uncertain whether the question put him in a better light or a worse.

It was recorded, but neither Lindenmeyer nor Creager gave him an answer. The role of questioner, here, was theirs.

'All right, Colin,' Lindenmeyer said for the third or fourth time, 'let's go over it again. This taxi-driver, this Armenian or Lebanese—'

LATER, lying stripped on the cot of a clean cell, he considered his position.

When he was brought down here he had not been thrown into the communal cell at the end of the corridor, which was crowded and stank and from which, as they passed, came catcalls and curses against the constable who was accompanying him, followed by gobs of spit, but he was alarmed just the same. It was a low throb in him, sign of some larger unrest that he had become part of.

He wished desperately that they had allowed him to wash. More than his assailant's blood, it was the man's smell, which once it got into his head might be ineradicable, that he felt all over him; the rancidness and close animal stink of self-loathing. He began to tremble with delayed shock. Not for the danger he had been in but for how close he had stood to an anguish so intense that the only escape from it was into self-extinction. When he did fall at last into a fevered sleep he was in a place where there were no walls; his sleep was open to the communal cell opposite, he was surrounded by broken mutterings and cries whose foul breath he took into his lungs and breathed out as protests that found no sound except as echoes in his skull.

At some point he woke, or half-woke. Three or four black youths were being dragged to the door of his cell, shouting obscenities; but the constable must have thought better of it and pushed them on. There was a scuffle. Hard blows against something soft or hollow. Then a violent eruption as the cell opposite burst into a howling, and again he had in his nostrils the odour of his assailant's sweat. It was overpowering. He started up, shouting, and his cry was immediately taken up in a renewed frenzy of catcalls and yells.

He did not sleep again. He lay stiff and still, aware of the exchange of heavy night-heat for the clearer heat of day. Light came, and with it the shrill clattering among palm fronds and fig trees of thousands of starlings.

'Right, mate,' the new duty-officer told him, 'you c'n have a bit 'v a wash. Inspector'll see yer.'

He stood in the open doorway, severely official, and let Colin pass.

The working day had begun. The cells were being unlocked. Bleary-eyed but subdued, the night's pick-ups had begun shuffling out: drunks, derelicts, young toughs, barefoot and with tattoos on their calves, who had been hauled out of fist fights just on closing time or from round the doors of discos, thin young Aborigines, one or two with dreadlocks – the agents, or victims or both, of a violence that was random but everywhere on the loose. You had only to step into the path of it to be picked up and whirled about and shattered. It was something he had always known about the place but had allowed himself to take for metaphor. He was being reminded again that it was fact.

He washed, when his turn came, at the dirty basin, and drew wet fingers through his hair.

In the metal mirror above the tap he barely recognized himself. The metal distorted, but there was also the puffed eye and thickened lip. He looked, he thought, like a dead ringer of himself who for thirty years had lived a different and coarser life – maybe even that of the man he had been mistaken for.

THE interrogation room appeared different in daylight. Larger. But the real difference was that Lindenmeyer and Creager had been pushed to the edges of it, one lounging in a chair by the typewriter, the other hunched into the window frame. The younger man who occupied the centre immediately offered Colin his hand. His name was McKinley.

'I'm sorry, Mr Lattimer,' he said, all affability, 'we've finally got things sorted out. You'll be free in just a minute.'

Without being obvious he made it clear that he knew quite well who he was dealing with, and might even, if pressed, have been able to produce a title.

Lindenmeyer and Creager watched closely, wearing faces that expressed different styles of contempt – whether for him or for their superior he could not guess.

Creager might have spent the remainder of the night in the derros' cell. His tiny blue eyes had disappeared into the beef of his cheeks. He kept hitching his belt over the roll of his belly. Lindenmeyer, too intelligent not to feel that this writer bloke and the inspector made an oaf of him, boiled with resentment. Whatever residue of violence the room contained came from him.

'The man's out of danger,' McKinley was telling Colin. 'Superficial wounds is what the report says. It wasn't a serious attempt.' He cleared his throat. 'Mind you, he's still pretty convinced that he's got some grudge against you.'

The hint of a question in his voice made Colin say very firmly, for perhaps the twentieth time in the last eight hours, 'I never saw the man in my life before.'

McKinley nodded.

'Well, don't concern yourself. On the evidence,' he said, as if evidence might not be the only thing to go by, 'we accept that. The man doesn't, that's all. We're waiting for the psychiatrist's report.'

Lindenmeyer and Creager were grinning. McKinley paused,

regarding him, Colin thought, with anticipation, as if, now that he was officially cleared, he might offer some private explanation of an affair that was still worryingly obscure. McKinley's interest at this point could be thought of as personal, literary – that was the suggestion – and Colin's obligation to explain, that of an author to a loyal but puzzled reader.

But Colin himself was in the dark. It might have helped, he thought, if he had had a name for the man he had struggled with, held close, beaten, and whose blood and sweat, mingled with his own, had discoloured the water in the dirty handbasin and gone swirling to join the rest of the city's scourings, the accumulated debris and filth of nearly a million souls.

What he had not been able to wash off was the claim that had been laid upon him. In some ward, in a hospital somewhere in the city, a man lay sedated, physically restrained perhaps, who still inwardly pursued him, consumed with resentment for the harm done to him by a shadowy third party to whom, Colin thought, he too was connected, but in ways so dark and undeclared that they might never be known.

But if McKinley did have a name, he did not offer it, and Colin knew that he could not ask.

'I'll just call your friend in,' he said, closing what had been for a moment an open silence.

Eric was outside and immediately turned to face them, substantial-looking in a suit and tie, and already preparing, Colin saw, to take charge. His face was a mixture of concern for an old friend – 'Are you okay, Colin?' – and prickly disdain for the ways of local officialdom.

McKinley too saw it, but stood back, too polite to let his irritation show. His attention was not on Eric but on a woman on the bench opposite, who looked up, and as she did so, met Colin's eye.

He knew immediately who she must be, and was aware too of

the inspector's awakened interest. He was on the watch. Not out of professional interest now, but with that curiosity about human behaviour and its shifts and by-ways that made him both a policeman and a reader.

She was blonde, and coarse but sexy. He took in the soiled tank-top, the feet, which were dirty, in their high-heeled, patent-leather sandals, and felt a little shameful kick of desire.

A smile, half-scornful, drew down the corner of her mouth. She had caught the spark of attraction in him that might have confirmed, to a practised onlooker like the inspector, that his assailant's suspicions had to this extent at least been entirely plausible. For a moment they made a triangle, a second one, this woman, the inspector and himself. The tension of the moment was felt by all three.

It was Eric who broke it. 'Come on, Colin,' he said. 'Let's get you out of here.'

So it was over – or almost. In moving too quickly away under the double gaze of the inspector and the woman, Colin stumbled, very nearly fell, and found himself caught and supported by an arm that shot out from nowhere and belonged, when he looked up, to a young man in a crash-helmet who had been waiting at the counter to report a theft.

'Hey, steady on.'

'Sorry,' Colin said as he righted himself. Then, 'Thanks.'

'She's right, mate.' The young man produced a grin that was all friendliness and good humour and a frankness that knew no guile.

'Come on,' Eric said, in a tone that suggested a growing apprehension at how accident-prone his new friend might be. 'I'll get you back to the hotel, we can ring Coralie from there.'

SAFELY back in his room at the hotel, he splashed cold water over his face, and as soon as he had recovered a little, rang London. Emma's voice was thick with sleep.

'I'm sorry,' he said. 'I just wanted to hear your voice.'

He closed his eyes, and her breathing in his ear was so close that she might have been lying half-curled against his body in the dark.

'What is it?' she asked. 'What time is it?'

'Nothing. It's nothing to worry about. Go on back to sleep.'

The closeness, the familiarity of her, collapsed the hemispheres, the vast spaces across which her voice was being projected towards him. With his eyes close-shut he could believe that the slight hissing he could hear in the gaps of her breathing came from the high-ceilinged room where she lay, their flat high up above Redcliffe Square, and felt himself settle in the stillness and order, even in its customary disorder, of their shared life: dishes left overnight in the sink, books on shelves, LPs, newspapers.

'Go back to sleep,' he said again. 'I'm fine. I just wanted to hear your voice.'

'No, it's nothing,' she was calling now, her head turned away from the mouthpiece. 'It's Colin. From Australia.'

That would be Marcus. He saw the boy standing in striped flannel pyjamas and his Manchester United jersey at the door to their room.

He was sixteen and diabetic, so used to his disease and its regimen that you were barely aware of it except for the chocolate biscuits he carried in the pockets of his coat. He liked to go to discos. He was so easy and serious and assured that Colin, who, in the three years that he and Emma had been together, had grown fond of the boy, was sometimes intimidated. He expected the young to be confused, as he had been.

'That was Marcus,' Emma told him unnecessarily. 'Are you sure you're all right?'

'Yes, I'm fine, I'll be there on Friday. Go on back to sleep. I'll ring in the morning.'

He listened for a moment after she hung up to the different quality of silence – which was no longer that of their bedroom and the warmer, reassuring spaces of the flat, but the white noise, the rubbing together in a soft, functional hissing, of a myriad random particles colliding and parting in the high wastes of air.

AT seven that evening, uneasily assured and with a puffiness about the lip that gave him a disreputable look, which must have been a puzzle to those readers of newspaper and magazine articles for whom he was always 'distinguished', he read to a modest gathering at a popular bookshop, then fielded the usual questions, some effusively respectful but others aggrieved. What did he think of the place? Why had it taken him so long to come back? How had his work suffered by his having abandoned, as they said, his roots? Still feeling battered, he moved to one of the vast plate-glass windows and looked out.

The city he knew, and in one part of himself still moved in, was out there somewhere, but out of sight, underground. Unkillably, uncontrollably green. Swarming with insects and rotting with a death that would soon once again be life, its salt light, by day, blinding to the eye and deadening of all thought, its river now, under fathoms of moonlight, bursting with bubbles, festering, fermenting.

Inescapable. Far from having put it too far behind him, he felt entangled, caught.

He thought of the flying foxes hanging in furry rows under the boughs of the Moreton Bay figs, the metho-drinkers on the Victoria golf-links, the teenage blacks and dropouts on their cots at the watchhouse or in gutters in the lanes off Mary and Margaret Streets. The frowsy blonde in the back room of a massage parlour, the taxi-driver with one hairy arm out the window, drumming impatiently on the roof. And in a darkened room somewhere, a man, restrained or sedated, who long after the scars had healed on his neck and chest would go on stalking down midnight pavements the one who had wronged him.

LATER, in the cool of a room nine storeys above the street, he fell into a reviving sleep and was for a time nowhere – or nowhere that can be found on any map.

He was standing at a street corner, lounging against a wall in the neon dark and watching the headlamps of a truck rise slowly between lightpoles over the crown of a hill. He did not move. Even when the truck drew level, stopped and he was called to. Till, being called a second time, he pushed away from the wall, ambled to the kerb, and setting his hand on the high cabin window, listened, shrugged his shoulders, looked to where others, already blindfold, were packed together in the open truck, and shrugged again. Then, blindfolded himself, he was hauled up to join them, and they began a long ride out through the sleeping suburbs towards wherever it was out there in the foothills that the green stuff, the dream stuff, was.

The truck came to a halt, high among insect voices. He shuffled to the edge of the tray, a little breathless. How long a drop was it? He put his hand out, feeling air. Then there was a hand. He had only to take it and launch off.

And now, in a stretch of time where before and after had no meaning, in which none of the things had yet occurred that had so shaken his world and none of the people who most mattered to him had yet left his life or come into it, or they had and he was not yet aware of it – in that neither before nor after, he was high up under the floorboards of the house, and though the light was almost gone, he knew that the pale stems in which he could see the endless pushing upwards of a liquid green were the stems of gladioli, and that the great weight of darkness in his arms, which was still warm, was Maxie. The heart he could feel beating had a worm in it but had not yet stopped. It still made a regular, reassuring thump against his ribs.

He heard them call. They were calling to him.

'Come on out now. Come out,' and a hand was stretched towards him.

But he would not for a while yet, for a good while yet, respond to the voices, or reach out and put his own into the outstretched hand.

Night Training

@/@

THE day Greg Newsome turned seventeen he joined the University Air Squadron. It was 1951. The memory of one war, which had been in progress all through his childhood, was still strong in him, gathering to it all the appealing mementoes and moods of those years, and the Cold War had recently thrown up another conflict, a smaller one, in Korea. War seemed to him, and to others like him, a natural thing. It galvanized people's energies and drew them to a pitch. It clarified meanings. It held you in the line of history. It also cleansed the spirit by offering occasions where mere animal energy and the noblest aspirations could meet at a point of vivid exultation, and mind and body, which at a certain age seem like divergent states of being, were instantly reconciled.

When Greg went to be medically examined he had to wait for more than an hour in a poky enclosure with walls of three-ply. There were a dozen other fellows there, on benches; he didn't know a single one of them. He plunged into his book, a Loeb

Classic. When he was called at last he had to strip and sit on a chair to one side of the examiner's desk.

The man was a civilian but with one of those handlebar moustaches that in those days still evoked the image of a fighter pilot in the war. He looked at Greg's birth date, then at Greg, and was silent. Greg blushed. It was odd to be sitting stark naked on a chair beside a desk with his flesh sticking to varnish. He hung on mentally to his Plato.

'So,' the doctor said, 'we've got around to you lot.' His face expressed a profound weariness.

ON their first camp three months later he was assigned to the Intelligence Unit and shared a hut with the other baby of the squadron, a country boy from Harrisville, Cam Brierly. They were so much the youngest that they took it in turns on official mess nights, when all the officers of the station were assembled, to be Mister Vice: that is, to reply to toasts and initiate the passing of the port. It was a role in which you appeared to be the centre of the occasion, but only in the clownish sense of being a king of fools.

They stuck together, he and Cam. Not because they had anything in common but to conceal from others their appalling innocence.

Their task by day was to catalogue and reshelve the station library, under the eye of the Chief Education Officer, Dave Kitchener, a cynical fellow who did nothing himself but lounge behind his desk and was by turns a bully and a tease. He resented having them fobbed off on him.

At night, after dinner, while other fellows got drunk, played darts or snooker, or sang round the piano in true wartime style, they tried, one after another, a series of exotic liqueurs of lurid colour and with enticing names: Curaçao, Crème de Menthe, Parfait d'Amour. They were sickly, every one.

The mess late at night got rowdy, then out of hand. Understanding, though they never admitted it, that if they hung around too long they would very likely become butts, for their youth was in itself ridiculous, they slipped away before eleven and were soon asleep.

O NE of the wildest figures at these nightly gatherings was Dave Kitchener, the officer who gave them such a hard time by day. A bit of an outsider with his fellow officers, he was always looking for trouble. When he got a few drinks under his belt he turned sarcastic, then aggressive, and went on the prowl; they had, more than once, caught him glaring in their direction. If he once got up, they thought, and came across, it would be to lash them with his tongue. They knew him by now. He couldn't be trusted to keep to the rules. He might pass muster in the office, and on official parade, but in the mess at night his uniform was loosened at the neck, and his hair, which was longer than permitted, fell uncombed over his brow. He had a sodden look.

Six or seven years back – Greg had the story from a fellow who had known him at Charters Towers when he was a geography master at All Souls – he had been caught climbing into the room of a woman from the sister school, Blackheath, and after a scandal that was quickly hushed up, they were both dismissed. One night when there were women in the mess, Air Force nurses, Dave Kitchener went up to one of them and threw a glass of beer in her face.

They had been in camp for two weeks when he appeared for the first time in their hut.

IT must have been between one and two in the morning. Greg stirred, aware of a presence in the room that registered itself first as a slight pressure on his consciousness, then on the mattress beside him. He woke and there he was, sitting on the edge of the bed. Just sitting. Quietly absorbed, as if he had come in, tired, to his own room and was too sleepy to undress.

He's made a mistake, Greg thought.

His cap was off, his tie loose, and there was a bottle in his hand.

Greg lay quiet. Nothing like this had ever happened to him before. He didn't know what to do. When the man realized at last that he was being watched, he turned, fixed his eyes on Greg, made a contemptuous sound deep in his throat, and laughed. He lifted the bottle in ironic salute. Then, reaching for his cap, which he had tossed carelessly on to the bed, he set it on his head, got to his feet and took a stance.

'All right, cadet,' he said. 'Get out of there.'

Greg was astonished.

'Didn't you hear? That was an order.' His nails flicked the stripes on his sleeve. 'Get your mate up. I said, get up!'

Greg rolled out of bed. He was out before he properly realized it. This must be a dream, he thought, till the cold air struck him. Skirting the officer, who stood in a patch of moonlight in the centre of the room, he crossed to Cam's bed and hung there in a kind of limbo, looking down at his friend. He still couldn't believe this was happening.

'Go on,' the man told him.

Cam was sound asleep, and Greg, still touched by a state that seems commonplace till you are unnaturally hauled out of it, was struck by something he had never felt till now: the mystery, a light but awesome barrier, that surrounds a sleeping man. Which is meant to be his protection, and which another, for reasons too deep to be experienced as more than a slight tingling at the hair-roots, is unwilling to violate.

Cam's head rested on the upper part of his arm, which was thrust out over the edge of the mattress. Under the covers his legs were moving, as if he were slowly running from something, or burrowing deeper into the dark.

Greg glanced across his shoulder at the officer, hoping, before this new breach was made, that he would reconsider and go away. But the man only nodded and made an impatient sound. Greg put his hand out. Gingerly, with just the tips of his fingers, he touched Cam's shoulder, then clasped it and shook.

But Cam was difficult. He put up a floppy arm and pushed Greg off. Even when Greg had got him at last into a sitting position he wasn't fully awake. Sleep was like a membrane he was wrapped in that would not break. It made everything about him hazy yet bright: his cheeks, his eyes when they jerked open. Greg began to be impatient. 'Come on, Cam, get up,' he whispered. 'Stop mucking about.'

The man, standing with the cap at a rakish angle, laughed and took a swig from his bottle.

'Wasser matter?' Cam muttered. The words were bubbly. ''S middle o' the night.'

Greg hauled him up, cursing, and propped him there: he kept giggling like a child and going loose. 'Cut it out,' Greg hissed, staggering a little in the attempt to hold him. He hadn't realized before what a spindly, overgrown fellow he was. But at least he was on his feet, if not yet fully present. Greg turned to the officer.

Dave Kitchener had been watching his struggles with a mixture of amusement and contempt. He seated himself, as before, on the edge of Greg's bunk, his legs apart, the cap pushed now to the back of his head, his feet firmly planted. He was enjoying himself.

'Right,' he said. 'Now. Get stripped.'

Greg was outraged. After all his exertions with Cam, it still wasn't finished. This is wrong, he told himself as he started on the buttons of his pyjama jacket. He shouldn't be wearing his cap that way. He shouldn't be sitting on my bed. He wrenched at the buttons in a hopeless rage, the rage a child feels at being unjustly punished, feeling it prickle in his throat. Tears, that meant. If he wasn't careful he would burst into tears. His concern now was to save himself from that last indignity. He lifted his singlet over his head, undid the cord of his pants. They were in winter flannels. In the mornings here, when you skipped out barefoot to take a piss, the ground was crunchy with frost.

Cam was still dazed. He stood but was reeling. Greg looked towards the officer; then, with deliberate roughness, began to undo the buttons on Cam's jacket.

'We've got to take them off,' he explained as to a three-year-old.

When they were naked Dave Kitchener had them drill, using a couple of ink-stained rulers. He kept them at it for nearly an hour.

He did not come every night. Three or four might pass and they would be left undisturbed, then Greg would be aware again of that change of pressure in the room.

After the first occasion there was no need for commands. As soon as Greg was awake, Dave Kitchener would rise, stand aside for him to pass, and Greg would go obediently to Cam's bed and begin the difficult exercise of getting him to his feet. It was always the same. Cam had to be dragged to the occasion. He resisted, he pushed Greg off. Laughing in his sleep in a silly manner and muttering sentences or syllables from a dialogue of which only the one side could be heard, he reeled and clung on.

Dave Kitchener showed no interest in these proceedings. They were Greg's affair. He left him to it. And because the officer no longer made himself responsible, Greg found all this intimate business of getting Cam out of bed and awake and stripped more repugnant than ever. Damn him! he thought – meaning Cam. He had come to see this peculiarity in the other boy, his reluctance to come awake, as a form of stubborn innocence. It set his own easy wakefulness in a shameful light. He resented it, and his resentment carried over into their dealings in the library as well. They began to avoid one another.

Meanwhile the waking and drilling went on. And afterwards, while they stood naked and shivering but at ease, the lectures.

EACH morning the squadron was broken up into specialist units, but in the afternoons after mess, they came together for a series of pep talks that were intended to develop a spirit of solidarity in them as well as providing an introduction to the realities of war. Some of these talks were given by men, bluff self-conscious fellows not much older than themselves, who were just back from the fighting in Korea. They made everything, even the rough stuff, sound like Red Rover or some other game, where getting a bloody knee, or your shirt torn, was the risk you took for being in it. One fellow told them that his liaison officers up there had been called Cum Suk and Bum Suk, then went on to describe the effects of something called napalm.

In the break between lectures they stood about smoking, or formed circles and tossed a medicine-ball.

DAVE Kitchener's lectures were of a different sort, and they came, after a time, to signify for Greg the real point of these midnight sessions, for which the rest, the dreamlike ritual of ordering and presenting arms, of turning left, right, about face, coming to attention, standing at ease and easy, was a mere preliminary, a means of breaking them down so that they would not resist. They drilled. Then they stood at ease, they stood easy, and Dave Kitchener, walking in slow circles around them, began.

After the formal hectoring of the bullring, the roars of official rage and insult that were a regular thing out there, Dave Kitchener's voice, which seldom rose above a whisper in the room, was unnerving. They felt his breath at moments on the back of their necks. Then, too, there was their nakedness. They were like plucked chooks – that's how Greg felt. Goose-pimpled with cold and half-asleep on their feet, they stood, while the voice wove round and round them.

'What I'm trying to do is wake you up to things. You're so wet behind the ears, both of you, you're pitiful! Have you got any idea how pitiful you look? Because your mothers love you and you've been to nice little private schools, you think you've got it made. That nothing can touch you. That you're covered by the rules. Well, let me tell you, lad, there *are* no rules. There's a war on out there, you're heading right for it, and there are no rules. Oh, I know that's not what they tell you in those jolly pep talks they give you. What I'm talking about is something different. The real war. The one that's going on all the time. Right here, now, in this room.' He laughed. Greg heard the spittle bubble on his tongue. 'The one where they've already got you by the balls.' He stood back, looked them over, turned away in disgust. 'You poor little bastards. You don't even know what I'm talking about, do you? You should see yourselves. You're pitiful. You're fucking pitiful. I'm wasting my time on you.'

He would go on like that for the best part of an hour, a mixture of taunts, threats, insults, concern, and blistering anger at the quality in them that most offended him, their naïve confidence in things; which he was determined to relieve them of, and which they were unable to give up – it belonged too deeply to the power they felt in themselves, the buoyancy and resistance of youth. Greg discovered after a time how to handle it. You did just what you were ordered to do down to the last detail, with scrupulous precision, as you never did out there on the bullring. Not in mockery of the thing itself – that would have been to enter into collusion with him, for whom this was already a mockery – but to mock his authority with its limits. Your body obeyed to the letter. The rest of you stayed away.

THEIR last day in camp was a passing-out parade. Several of the older fellows were to get commissions, which would entitle them to wear their caps without the virginal white band. Three of them were getting wings.

The bullring dazzled in the sun; they sweated in their heavy uniforms. A band played. The voices of the drill sergeants leapt out and they responded. 'Stand at ease, stand easy.' Dave Kitchener was there, his cap straight, his collar fastened. He saluted when the others did.

Watching from his company in the ranks, Greg was puzzled by a kind of emptiness in himself, a lack of connection with all this. Something in him had moved away, and might have been lounging off there in the shade of one of the huts, with its spine against a wall and the curl of a smile on its lips, bored now with the whole show: these movements that were so fixed and refined that the discipline they embodied seemed like another nature, the swing of their arms that brought the rifles down, the clunking of boots, their bodies aligned and responding as one to snapped commands. His own body was too constant for him not to remember that he had performed these movements smartly elsewhere. He had an impulse to make some deliberate error and break the line. He closed his lids and swallowed. 'Eyes right!' The image that fixed itself in his head was of the bullring empty, lit only by the moon, with the bluish shadow of the flag-mast, also empty, falling far across it.

H E saw Cam Brierly only once in the following year. They were no longer the youngest, and since that had been the only thing in common between them, they were free to keep apart. They never spoke of Dave Kitchener or made any mention of the night training. In time, those shameful episodes took on a quality of unreality that belonged to the hour, somewhere between one and three in the morning, when they had taken place: the hours of regulated dark when they, like all those others laid out in officers' huts and barracks, should have been safe under the blankets pursuing innocuous dreams. It was almost, in the end, as if they had been. Greg's anger faded in him. So did the sense of injury he felt. When sometimes, in the following years, he thought of Dave Kitchener he understood, from the midst now of that other war he had spoken of, what it was that had fired and frustrated the man. He felt a kind of pity for him.

It was about this time that he had a dream. He was standing once again beside Cam Brierly's bed, looking down at the sleeping figure from a height, a distance of years, and with a mixture of tenderness and awe that arrested every possibility of movement in him. He could no more have leaned down and broken the other's sleep at that moment than woken himself. Some powerful interdiction was on him. He looked back over his shoulder and said firmly: 'No!'

But the one who had been there in his dream was not there to hear it. He found himself staring into darkness, fully awake.

Sally's Story

◎◎

SALLY Prentiss was one of those girls who in the last days of the Vietnam War were known as 'the widows'.

For a week or ten days as required they would set up in a one-bedroom apartment – thoughtfully supplied with candles in a kitchen drawer for intimate evenings and a box of geraniums on the sill – with an American GI or marine (sometimes an officer) who, for months amid the welter and din of war, had been hoarding some other dream than the ones that were generally on offer at the Cross: an illusion of domestic felicity in the form of a soft-mouthed girl and the sort of walk-up city-style living that is represented by an intercom and a prohibition against the playing of loud music after eleven o'clock.

To lie in until midday while the sun shone in on the bed-covers, then go off to the beach or an afternoon movie, then come back and fuck – but in a leisurely way, with no need to hurry, and with the luxury sometimes, which is another sort of pleasure, of not having to fuck at all – this was the ordinary bliss they had set their sights on, a rehearsal for the settled life to come, when, their term of duty over, they would have no other obligation than to get pleasurably and without effort from one day to the next.

Sally Prentiss was an actress. That is, she was preparing to audition for NIDA. She had taken up this work because it paid better than anything else she had been offered. At just nineteen she was very aware that she had no real experience of life and she thought this might supply it. She was a down-to-earth person who knew how to stick up for herself; she did not think it would be damaging. She would only be doing it for a few months, and the men who wanted this sort of arrangement – or so she thought – would be nicer than the average, and since they would be pretending while they played house that everything was normal, would make fewer demands. They *were* nice for the most part, but she was wrong about the damage, and she was wrong about the demands as well.

They came in every variety, these boys, these men.

Some of them were barely house-trained. They licked the flat of their knives when they were eating – she pretended not to notice; they did not know how to wash properly or when they should change their socks. 'Oh Delilah,' she said to herself in a voice of commiseration, 'not another one!' She had a whole cast of voices that she used for bucking herself up or giving herself a good talking-to, or for commenting, in a half-mocking way, on the irony of things and the rebounds and reversals that made up her world.

As for the demands – of course, all some of them wanted, or thought they wanted, was sex, laid on and guaranteed at any hour of the day or night. A wife out of the porno magazines. But even these boys wanted sometimes to just hang in the doorway and, in a proprietorial way, watch her do something as simple as make her face up in the bedroom mirror or wriggle into her jeans.

They would come up behind her while she was washing dishes at the sink, shoes off, hair damp with sweat, and, slipping their arms around her waist, rock her gently against them to an unheard tune – a moment, sweetly evocative, out of an old movie they had seen on TV. Or, with an ease that suggested an intimacy so long established that it no longer vibrated with even a hint of the provocative, walk in while she was in the bath, lower the toilet seat, and have a good old-fashioned talk.

What many of them wanted was to have reinforced the illusion of mastery. To a point sometimes just short of brutality. But there were times when even these fellows wanted to be relieved of all that and just lie back and be petted.

Then there were the ones – she got to recognize them after a bit – who just sat around all day in their undershorts and never left the flat. They were uncomfortable with air and sunlight, or had seen too much of it. One big foot up on the edge of the coffee-table, eyes glued to the TV, downing can after can of beer, they ignored her; but at every moment, whatever she was doing, kept her in view. However far off she might move, she was never quite out of reach. Idly, almost abstractedly, without taking their eyes off the game they were watching, they would put a hand out, and with the same easy affection for the body's demands with which they might shift themselves more comfortably in their undershorts or scratch their heel, take possession of her neck and push her down.

They were almost completely cut off from speech, these fellows. Their denial of words, like their body smell, was something they imposed, on the room, on her, with a satisfaction they were barely aware of since it had to do entirely with themselves.

She put up with it but was filled with rage. This pleased some of them, though they might also use it later as an excuse for complaint, then violence. The blows were real enough, but the words they found to spit out at her, the routine obscenities, were half-hearted, a formula for keeping them excited, for reminding themselves that she was there.

God, she thought, what a nightmare! Imagining years of marriage on such terms.

Then there were the ones who felt an obligation to teach her things. Very solemn and little-mannish, their freshly scrubbed faces intent on the task of relieving her of some aspect, suddenly revealed, of female ignorance, they would deliver long, sometimes incomprehensible lectures on politics or the Market or the workings of some bit of equipment they had fallen in love with, while she, barely attending, sipped at a Coke or did her nails.

Usually this sort of boy did not care to be interrupted. All she had to do was keep nodding. But one or two of them wanted her to repeat what she had learned, and there were others who liked her to argue, but when she did would get mad and shout at her. This aroused some of them. To the point where they would all of a sudden forget that they were engaged in the business of instruction and want to fuck – right there on the living-room rug.

There was no way of guessing beforehand the quite ordinary things that would turn them on.

One moment they would be as still as a pond, everything would be relaxed and easy between them. The next they would have dived into themselves and be staring. Some gesture she had made, something she had said or done, had made her suddenly alive to their senses, provoked in them a rush of blood. What alarmed her was that for her there was no connection; she had felt nothing herself and almost never knew what it was.

There were times, faced with this impersonal power she possessed, when she wanted, quite simply, to run. But mostly what she felt was a kind of pity. They were so utterly at the mercy, these boys, of their needs; and they hated it, some of them, and could convince themselves, even while they were fiercely pushing into her, that *she* was the source of this fever they were afflicted with, this animal dependency without which they might have been hard and pure and self-sufficient.

They were just boys, she knew that, but they made her mad. She often quarrelled with them and said things that were mocking and cruel, but only in her head. Laying the responsibility for their failings on her, making her responsible for their weakness, was unfair. They did not play fair.

But the quality in them that she found hardest to live with was their restlessness. They were always looking at their watches and could not settle. Something was always missing. And this was just what they had feared. That having survived and come so far, the thing they had come for might still be out of reach, or be happening elsewhere, and at every moment time was passing. 'Peter, Paul and Mary,' she whispered, 'save our souls!'

But she saw at last that this was only part of a larger fear, and she learned after a time never to look, never to really look, into their eyes. What she saw there when she did was scary and might be catching. She wanted to keep clear. But there was no way of touching them and keeping clear.

She had thought, since they had been through so much and were *boys*, were *men*, that they would by now have learned to deal with it; or that being here in the quietness of the city, with a glint of sunlit water at the end of the street, they might forget. But they did not. It wasn't a mental thing. So long as their body was there, big and pulsing with heat, so was the fear. They brought it to bed with them, in dreams from which they woke shouting, and the only thing then that might drive it off was sex. Terrifyingly possessed, they thrashed and sweated in the effort to push their body through to the other side, gasping at the limit of their breath, crying out into her mouth. And when they subsided and lapsed immediately into unconsciousness, it was a dead man's weight that was on her, a dead man's sweat she was drenched with.

All this, she came to understand, was why so few girls were willing to do this work and why those who did the same work, but on a one-time or one-night basis, held them in contempt. They gave too much of themselves: it was indecent. And as 'widows', they carried with them the taint of death.

She had thought this was ridiculous when she first heard it. Mere superstition. She thought she could outface it. But more and more now she had her doubts, especially in the last days of an engagement, when she had to deal with the ways – different in each case – in which these boys came to accept that their time was at an end. The war wasn't over. All they had done was step for a while out of the immediate line of it.

They paid the price then for their escape into make-believe, and she for having let herself, as she did at times, get too close. But how could she help it?

In a moment when her guard was down, when one of them was tickling her ear with some breathy story of the small town he came from, she would get a glimpse – that's all it took – into the odd, individual life of him; at the small naked creature in there, beyond the boastfulness and swagger, that was helpless and soft as a worm.

Often enough it was something physical that did it, the mother-of-pearl whiteness of an appendix scar, or some blemish she had not seen before, and which close up filled the whole of her view. Suddenly a body she had managed till now to touch without touching was *there*, heavy with its own meaty poundage, and hot, and real. It made their last moments together, if she did not deal sternly with herself, very nearly unbearable. As if, in allowing his body to lay itself bare to her, in her touching of it, there, and there, it was death itself that he had made himself open to, and what she was feeling out in him was the entry-place of a future wound.

As for the partings themselves, they too could take any form, and though they were final enough, were not always the end.

In some cases, the boy had already begun to leave a day or more beforehand, moving away in his head. All she had to do then was stay quiet and small while he got on with it. Others avoided the actual moment. Leaving her curled up in bed, they would pretend to be slipping out as usual to get the paper or a packet of cigarettes. She would lie there waiting to hear him lift his bags, which had been sitting all night in the hallway, then hold her breath for the last clicking of the latch.

But some wanted to believe that this was only the beginning. They would write, they would be back. She smiled and nodded, stirring her coffee with too much vigour. She hated to lie, but let herself cry a little, and her tears after a moment were real.

Then there were the ones who put on a turn. Like spoiled kids, toddlers. Big-shouldered in their freshly laundered shirts, they would sit beside their bags looking so plaintive, so stricken, that she had to pull the sheet over her head to save herself from the awfulness of it. You saw so nakedly what was being snatched away from them.

With the sheet pulled close over her head she would hear him deep-breathing out there, pumping himself up. Huh huh huh, on ten now!

She began to feel haunted. By so much that remained unfinished, unresolved in her relations with this or that one of them.

A phrase would come back to her, or a look, that was so sunny, so touched with ease and well-being, that she thought it must belong to some boy she had known back home. Then she would remember. It was one of them. Jake, or was it Walt, or Kent, or Jimmy? So this is what it means, she thought, to be a widow. She felt as if she had already, in just a few months, discovered things that made her older than the oldest woman alive. She had used up too many of her lives, that is what it was, in these phantom marriages.

At school last year their English teacher, Miss Drury, had given them a poem to crit. 'To speak of the woe that is in marriage' it was called. It was American. Modern.

She was good at English. It was her best subject. 'Woe', she had argued, was old-fashioned and melodramatic, a poet's word. Now she saw that the feeling it carried, the weight in it of all that was human and hopeless, made it utterly right. She knew now what it meant. Pay a fine of one hundred dollars, she told herself, and return to Go! She considered writing to Miss Drury and telling her of this late enlightenment, though not the means by which she had come to it.

PERHAPS it was a recollection of simpler days, of HSC English and Miss Drury, that made her decide to take time off and spend a week or two at home.

But by the second day she remembered again why she had left.

Her mother worked at a check-out counter in the one-storeyed main street of the little country town, where all the cars were angle-parked to the kerb and everyone knew one another and there was nothing to do.

Boys, as soon as they were old enough, congregated at the pub, spilling out barefoot in stubbies and football jerseys on to the pavement, which was lined with empty glasses. The girls, over-dressed and with too much make-up, walked up and down from one of the two coffee-shops to the other, much preoccupied with their hair, too brightly on the lookout for occasions they feared might never occur. At home, after work, her mother took photographs of little kids in their school uniforms with slicked-down wetted hair or all decked out in white for their first communion, then, at the weekend, of wedding groups. She had a studio and dark-room on the closed-in back verandah and rented a window in the main street, full of examples of her work: smiling couples, good-looking boys in uniform, cute tots.

Her younger brother, Brian, who was fourteen, spent all his time in the camouflage battledress of his school cadet corps, including a khaki net that he wore round his shoulders like a shawl.

Sometimes he wrapped his head in it and stalked the corridors of the house in his big boots, moving warily through an atmosphere of damp heat and dripping bamboo while the boards under the linoleum creaked. He even wore the uniform when he was practising shots out in the yard at their basketball ring, and once, looking into his room, she saw him, his face swathed in the net, sitting crouched under the desk-lamp, doing his maths homework. Did he sleep in it?

Only once did she see him when he wasn't in full rig. He had taken the jacket off to chop wood in the yard. She was shocked by his thinness and by the whiteness of his hairless arms and chest.

At breakfast she asked, 'Don't you ever take it off?'

He grunted, his face in a bowl of cornflakes.

'Does he ever wash?' she asked her mother.

Her mother looked at him and frowned, as if she were seeing this warrior who had seated himself at her kitchen table for the first time.

'Brian,' she said wearily, 'a shower! Tomorrow, eh? Did you hear what I said?'

'Huh,' he grunted.

Her sister, Jess, who was two years younger but the same height, worshipped him. She longed for a uniform and was sometimes allowed to wrap her head in the camouflage net while they practised shots at the ring. They never stopped sniping at one another and appealing to her mother to adjudicate.

ON the Saturday she went off with her mother to a wedding. In the yard of the reception hall at the School of Arts they ran into Mrs Preston, who was a guest at the wedding and the mother of her oldest friend, Jodie. She and Jodie had been at school together.

'Oh, didn't you hear?' Mrs Preston told her. 'Jodie's married. They're living out at Parkes. Clive – her husband – is in the railways.'

'And Jodie?' Sally asked. She had been the wildest of their group. She was surprised to hear that Jodie was married.

Mrs Preston looked beatific. 'Jodie,' she told them, 'is getting on with her cake decoration.'

Today's wedding, as usual up here, was a very grand affair: three bridesmaids attended by groomsmen in suits of the same pastel blue. All shoulders, and uncomfortable with their buttonholes and formal bow ties, they had played rugby with the groom. One of them, Sally noticed, fooled about a lot. He was a broadfaced, well-set-up fellow with a full mouth, but otherwise very square and manly. He had a thatch of blond hair that would not stay down, and kept beating at it with the flat of his hand. He got drunk on the cheap champagne and made bawdy remarks that people laughed at, and chatted up all the girls, and was at every moment in a state of high excitement, but in the photographs when they were developed looked dark, almost surly. This was surprising.

'Who's this?' she asked her mother.

'Oh, that's Brad Jenkins; don't you remember him?'

'No,' she said. 'I don't think so. Should I?'

'Works down at McKinnon's Hardware. Used to work for Jack Blade at the service station. Don't you remember him?'

'No,' she said.

'Poor boy, his wife left him. Lives out Dugan way with two little kiddies. It can't be much fun.'

'Why?' she asked, examining the photo. 'Why did she leave?'

'Who knows? Just packed up one day and when he got home she was gone. People say she ran off with a fellow she was engaged to before Brad. You know, she got pregnant to Brad, and—' Her mother consulted the photograph. 'Maybe he isn't as nice as he looks,' she said. 'Sometime these happy-go-lucky fellers—'

She didn't finish. She was thinking, Sally knew, of their father, who had been nice-looking and charming enough but grew sullen when there were no more hearts to win, and more and more disappointed with himself, and angry with them, and beat their mother, and at last, when they were still quite small, took off.

Sally, with her new understanding of these things, threw her arms around her mother, who was too surprised by this burst of affection to resist.

'Lordy, Lordy,' Sally said to herself in the old black mammy's voice she used for one set of exchanges with herself, 'life is *saaad*.'

IN the afternoons she had taken to going for long walks over the low, rather treeless hills. It pleased her, after so many months in the city, to be in the open again, alone and with no one to consider but herself.

The air in these late spring days had a particular softness. There were birds about, there was the scent of blossom. She felt a lightening of her spirits that was more, she thought, than just a response to the soft weather. She was beginning to recover some of her old good humour in the face of what life presented, its sly indignities. The errors she had made need not, after all, be fatal. 'Things will turn out all right, I'll survive. I'm young, I'm tougher than I look.'

This was the way she argued with herself as she strode out under the high clouds, with the rolling landscape before her of low hills and willow-fringed creeks and their many bridges.

One day, when she was out later than usual and had turned back because the sky far to the west had darkened and was growling, she was overtaken on the white-dust road by a Ford Falcon that tooted its horn, went past, then came to a halt and stood waiting for her to catch up. A dirty-blond head appeared at the window. 'Want a lift?'

'No thanks,' she called, still twenty yards off. 'I'm walking.'

'You'll get drenched,' the voice told her. 'Gunna be a storm.'

When she came level she saw who it was. She might not have recognized him without the blue suit and groomsman's bow tie, but it was him all right. Same unruly head of hair, same look of broad-faced amusement.

'That's all right,' she told him. 'I'll risk it.'

He looked at her, his eyes laughing. 'Okay,' he said, 'suit yourself. We don't mind, do we, Lou?'

She saw then that there was a child in the back, a boy about four years old, and a baby strapped in beside him and slumped sideways, sleeping.

'No,' the boy shouted, 'we don't mind. We got ourselves, eh?' He laughed and repeated it. It was a formula.

'That's right,' the man said.

'Hi,' said Sally, ducking her head to be on a level with the boy.

'Hi,' the boy said, suddenly shy.

They looked at one another for a moment, then he said, shouting: 'Hey, why don't you ride with us? We're not goin' far.'

'Where?' she asked, 'where are you going?'

'Anywhere! We're ridin' the baby. She likes it, it stops 'er screamin'. We just ride 'er and she stops. Anywhere we like. All over. We like havin' people ride with us, don't we, Brad?'

'Sometimes,' the man said. 'It depends.'

'We like girls,' the boy shouted.

The first drops of rain began to fall. They bounced in big splashes off the roof of the car.

'All right,' Sally said, 'I'll ride with you for a bit,' and she ran round the back of the car and got in.

'Well,' he said to the boy, 'we got lucky, eh?'

'We did,' the boy crowed, 'this time we got lucky.'

'Brad Jenkins,' the man told her, starting the car up. 'And that's Lou and Mandy.'

'I'm four,' the boy announced, 'an' Mandy's one. Nearly. Our mum ran off an' left us. He's our dad.'

She looked at the man. Oh Delilah, that mouth! she thought. He lifted an eyebrow and gave a slow grin. 'Reuters,' he said, 'all the news as soon as it happens. That's enough, eh, Lou? We don't want to give away *all* our secrets.'

'What secrets?' the boy shouted. 'What secrets, Daddy? Have we got secrets?'

'It's true,' he told her, still grinning. 'No secrets.'

The boy looked puzzled. Something was going on here that he didn't get. 'Hey,' he said, 'you didn't tell us your name.'

'Sally,' she told him. And added for the man's benefit, 'Prentiss.'

'I know,' he said. 'Jumbo's wedding.'

Almost immediately the heavens opened up and water began pouring into her lap. Not just a few drops, but a torrent.

'Sorry,' he said.

She shook her head. There was not much use complaining. The car swooped up and down the low hills.

'Hey, Brad,' the boy shouted over the sound of the storm, 'are we gunna take Sally to our house? Like the last one?'

'Steady on,' the man told him. 'She'll think we're kidnappers.'

'We are. We're kidnappers.'

'Don't worry,' he told her seriously. But she wasn't worried. It amused her to think of him riding round the countryside letting Lou do the talking for him, using the kids as bait. She didn't expect to find herself tied up at the back of a barn.

'He goes on like that all the time. Non-stop.'

'What?' The boy shouted. 'Was that about me?'

'Yes it was,' the man told him. 'I said you talk too much.'

'I do, don't I?' the boy said. He was very pleased with himself. 'I'm a chatterbox.'

'Okay, now, a bit of silence, eh? While we work out what we're doin'. You're soaked,' he told Sally. 'We could get you some dry clothes if you like. I could take you back after we've eaten. We'd be goin' out anyway t' get the baby to sleep— No, Lou,' he told the boy, who was trying to interrupt, 'I'll handle it. It's true, we *would* like it. I'm a pretty good cook.'

She wasn't taken in by any of this and he didn't expect her to be. Part of his charm, she saw, was that he expected you to see through him and become complicit in what all this playfulness, with its hidden urgencies, might lead to. But nothing else had happened to her in the last week.

'Okay,' she said. 'But you're looking after me, eh, Lou?'

'Am I? Am I, Brad? What for?'

'It's all right, mate,' he told him, 'she's jokin',' and he gave her a bold, shy look that was meant to disguise with boyish diffidence his easy assurance that she was not.

When they got there it proved to be a house on wheels, a portable barrack-block for workers on the line. Long and narrow, like a stranded railway carriage, it consisted of a dozen rooms all of the same size along a single corridor, with a kitchen unit at one end and a shower and a couple of toilets at the other. The rain had stopped as suddenly as it had begun, and the land, all washed and dripping, glowed under a golden sky.

'Well,' he said, 'this is it – nice, eh? We aren't cramped. Lots of room for expansion, if you'd like to move in. We can put up any number. We could open a hotel.'

Only four of the rooms were in use. The others, when she looked in, were thick with dust, the little square windows grimed with months, maybe years, of muck. One or two of them had old pin-ups on the walls. Another was piled with dusty cartons and magazines, and there were tools, several shovels and a pick or two in a pile in one corner.

'That's it,' he told her; 'have a poke around. I'll find something for you to put on in a minute while we dry your clothes.'

It was true. She was soaked. Her hair was dripping.

He was kneeling while he got Lou's wet shoes off. The baby was gurgling in an armchair.

'Sorry,' he said; 'take a towel. In that basket there – it's clean – and dry your hair. Children can't wait.'

After a minute, with the children settled: 'You watch baby for a bit,' he told Lou and, soft-footed in his socks, led Sally two doors down the corridor to a bedroom.

As soon as she stepped in, though he was careful to leave the door open, she felt the change in him; a heightening of his physical presence, a heat that glowed under his clothes, out of the open-necked shirt, and a wet-grass smell that was his excited sweat. She recalled what her mother had said: 'Two kids — that can't be much fun,' and was impressed by how easily her mother had found, in that word fun, just the light in which he should be looked at. What was essential in him, what you might need to take most seriously in him, was a capacity he had for being light-spirited, for making himself easy with the world.

'Well,' he said, breaking the tension between them, 'let's see what we've got.'

He found a pair of jeans in one drawer — his, she guessed, but they were clean enough — and among a jumble of T-shirts and jumpers in another, a woollen shirt, also his. He put his face into it and smelled to see if it was clean.

'Okay? Will they do?' he asked. 'I've got t' look after the baby now.' He hovered a moment, hesitant, apologetic, appealing to her to understand that he was not entirely free.

She closed the door behind him, but it was unnecessary really, and as soon as she did so she knew it was not to preserve her own privacy but so that she could peek a little into his. She changed quickly, then opened the door of the wardrobe.

Dresses, all neatly on hangers, and at the bottom a pile of shoes. In a drawer, jeans, shirts, all ironed and folded. His wife's clothes. Why hadn't he offered her something from here?

But she could see why. All this was untouched.

And what had she expected? To find them torn from their hangers and ripped? She felt a sadness in these things. In their emptiness. In their remaining just as the woman had left them, untouched. No, not untouched — she could imagine him opening the wardrobe and letting his hand move among them. Undisturbed. His own things, as she had seen when he found the shirt for her, were a mess.

She opened the drawer again, took up one of his T-shirts and held it to her face; saw the girlie magazine underneath, and the stiff, crumpled handkerchief.

'How's it going?' he called.

'Fine,' she said, closing the drawer.

'We'll toss these in the drier,' he said, when she emerged with her pile of wet clothes.

'I will! I will!' Lou shouted, and rushed to take them from her.

'It's okay,' he said, 'he knows how t' work it. I've got to bath the baby. Do you mind? Then I'll get us some tea.'

She watched while he sat the baby in a tub of warm water and washed her, supporting her very gently with one hand while he soaped and splashed with the other. He spoke to the baby, who crowed and gurgled, soft-talking her, and was absorbed. The habitual nature of what he was doing absorbed him and for moments at a time he seemed unaware of her presence. But at others he grew self-conscious, and the soft-talk, the way he handled the baby, she felt, was for her. Or perhaps it was simply that she was aware of *him*.

The jeans she wore, which were too big for her, were his. So was the shirt. Her own clothes were tumbling away in the drier.

Lou had come back. With the baby's fresh clothes in his lap, he was sitting very quietly watching them both. He too was subdued.

'Is she gunna stay?' he asked at last.

The man cast her one of his shy looks. 'I don't know,' he said. 'Why don't you ask her.'

'*Are* you?' the boy asked.

'We'll see,' she said.

The man turned away, but was smiling, she knew, and, holding the baby high, smacked a kiss on its wet belly. The baby laughed.

'Okay, Lou,' he said when the child was dried and set down, 'you can take over.'

'We're a team,' he told her.

'Oh, I can see that,' she said.

SHE did stay, and did not hold it against him that he was so obviously pleased with himself, and so eager to show how good he was – he was – and that it wasn't because of *that* that his wife had left.

What was it then? she wondered. Why did she? Would she too find out?

Lying awake beside him, this almost stranger with his warmth against her, listening to the depth of his breathing, she was aware of the watchers she would have to deal with: the ghostly versions of Hedda and Rosalind and Blanche Du Bois waiting silently in the dark for her breath to release them. Behind the flimsy pine door of the wardrobe, just feet away, the rows of empty frocks.

Then there was the hurt she had felt in him. She could heal that. It seemed to her, at this moment, that she wanted nothing more in the world than to be his healing. She did not see, or not immediately, that his presenting himself to her in this light, with so much tremulous need, and when he felt her response to it, so much commanding passion, might be her healing as well.

Sometime in the night she woke to find him gone, and when he came back again he had the baby.

'Sorry,' he whispered, as he set it down in the bed between them. 'Do you mind?' He lay down again holding the child close to his chest, cradling its head.

So there was that, too.

She began to laugh.

'What is it?' he asked; 'what's so funny? She won't be in the way. You go on back t' sleep. I'm used to it.' And reaching across the baby, he had another hand for her, his fingers gently stroking her cheek.

Lordy, Lordy, she said to herself, looking at the two of them, the rough thatch of his blond head, the baby nestling into the warmth of him, snuffing his scent, burrowing deep into the familiar bulk of him.

Life is so—

But she was not sure that she believed, quite yet, in such happy turnabouts, and feared it might be tempting fate if she were to find a word, a new one, to finish the phrase. Instead she too snuggled down and let herself float free on the unloaded breath.

Jacko's Reach

@⁄@

So it is settled. Jacko's Reach, our last pocket of scrub, has been won for progress. It is to be cleared and built on. Eighteen months from now, after the usual period of mud pies and mechanical shovels and cranes, we will have a new shopping mall, with a skateboard ramp for young daredevils, two floodlit courts for night tennis and, on the river side, a Heritage Walk laid out with native hybrids. Our sterner citizens and their wives will sleep safe at last in a world that no longer offers encouragement to the derelicts who gather there with a carton of cheap wine or a bottle of metho, the dumpers of illegal garbage, feral cats, and the few local Aborigines who claim an affinity with the place that may or may not be mystical.

Those four and a half acres were an eyesore – that's the council's line: openly in communication, through the coming and going of native animals and birds, or through seeds that can travel miles on a current of air, with the wilderness that by fits and starts, in patches here and great swathes of darkness there, still lies like a shadow over even the most settled land, a pocket of the dark unmanageable, that troubles the sleep of citizens by offering a point of re-entry to memories they have no more use for – to unruly and unsettling dreams. Four and a half acres.

Boys riding past it on their way to school are caught by a sudden impulse, and with a quick look over their shoulder, turn in there and are gone for the day on who knows what adventures and escapades.

Driving slowly past it, you see a pair of boots sticking out from under a bush. At eight-thirty in the morning! A drunk, or some late-night rover who has been knocked on the head and robbed. A flash of scarlet proclaims the presence of firetails lighting the grass.

Jacko's Reach: once known, and so marked on older maps, as Jago's. How, and at what point, by what slip of the tongue or consonantal drift, did the name lurch backwards into an earlier, not-quite-forgotten history, so that the white man's name became a black one and the place reverted, if only in speech, to its original owner's? Jacko's.

For as long as anyone can remember the people who had a legal right to the Reach, and are responsible for its lying unkept and unimproved, are Sydneysiders, but there are no Jacks or Jagos among them. They themselves have fallen back to a single remnant, a Miss Hardie of Pymble, who claims to have been a pupil of Patti, speaks with a German accent, and sold Jacko's over the telephone, they say, for a song.

It is a place you have to have seen and been into if you are to have any grasp of it. Most of all, you have to have lived with it as the one area of disorder and difference in a town that prides itself on being typical: that is, just like everywhere else. Or you have to have been hearing, for as long as you can recall, the local stories about the place, not all of them fit to be told – which does not mean that they are not endlessly repeated. Or you have to have lost something there – oh, years back. A little Eiffel Tower off a charm bracelet, or your first cigarette lighter, which you have never given up hope of kicking up again, and go searching for in sleep. Or you have to have stumbled there on something no one had warned you of.

Back before the First World War, two bullockies (they must have been among the last of their kind) settled a quarrel there. No one knows what it was about, but one party was found, the next day, with his skull smashed. The other had disappeared. The bullocks, no longer yoked to the wagon, had been left to wander.

Then, two days later, the second bullocky turned up again, hanging by his belt from a bloodwood. An eight-year-old, Jimmy Dickens, out looking for a stray cow and with the salt taste of porridge in his mouth and that day's list of spellings in his head, looked up and saw, just at eye-level, a pair of stockinged feet, and there he was, all six feet of him, pointing downward in the early light. Old Jimmy was still telling the story, in a way that could make the back of your neck creep, fifty years later, in my youth.

The facts of the case had got scrambled by every sort of romantic speculation, but it was the awe of that dumbstruck eight-year-old as he continued to look out, in a ghostly way, through the eyes of the gaunt old-timer, that was the real story. That, and the fact that it was still there, the place, and had a name. You could go out yourself and take a look at it. That particular patch of Jacko's, that tree, had been changed for ever, and become, for all of us who knew the story, the site of something you could touch. A mystery as real as the rough bark of the tree itself, it could change the mood you were in, and whatever it was you had slipped in there to get away from or do.

Well, that's Jacko's for you.

When I was seven or eight years old we used to play Cops and

Robbers there. It seemed enormous. Just crossing it from the main road to the river gave you some idea, at the back of your knees, of the three hundred million square miles and of Burke and Wills.

Later it became the place for less innocent games, then later again of games that were once again innocent, though some people did not think so. Jacko's became a code-word for something as secret as what you had in your pants: which was familiar and close, yet forbidden, and put you in touch with all the other mysteries.

The largest of those you would come to only later; in the meantime, Jacko's, just the word alone, fed your body's heated fantasies, and it made no odds somehow that the scene of those fantasies was a place you had known for so long that it was as ordinary as your own back yard. It was changed, it was charged. And why shouldn't it be? Hadn't your body worked the same trick on you? And what could be more familiar than that?

What Jacko's evoked now was not just the dusty tracks with their dried leaves and prickles that your bare feet had travelled a thousand times and whose every turning led to a destination you knew and had a name for, but a place, enticing, unentered, for which the old name, to remain appropriate, had to be interpreted in a new way, as if it had belonged all the time to another and secret language. Girls especially could be made to blush just at the mention of it, if your voice took on a particular note. For them too it had a new interest, however much they pretended.

Those four and a half acres, dark under the moon on even the starriest nights, could expand in the heat of Christmas and the months towards Easter till they filled a disproportionate area of your head.

On sultry nights when you had all the sheets off, they suggested a wash of air that could only be fresher and cooler on the skin, a space you could move in with the sort of freedom you had known away back when you were a kid. You walked out there in your sleep and found it crowded. There were others. You met and touched. And those who were bold enough, or sufficiently careless of their reputation, or merely curious about the boundary of something too vague for the moment to be named, actually went there, in couples or foursomes. They weren't disappointed, exactly, but they came out feeling that their mothers had exaggerated. There was no danger, except in what people might make of it through talk, and about that their mothers had not exaggerated, not at all.

Valmay Mitchell was thirteen. She got no warning from her mother because she did not have one. She lived with her father in an old railway hut out on the line.

Every fellow of my generation knows Valmay's name. If she were to come back here, to take a last look at Jacko's for instance before it goes under for ever, she would be astonished at her fame.

She was a plain, blonde little thing who left school in the sixth grade. She wore dresses that were too big for her, went barefoot, and her one quality that anyone recalls was her eagerness to please. She would do anything – that was the news. Then one day, when we were all in the seventh grade, she disappeared. She was nowhere to be found.

People immediately thought the worst. Valmay Mitchell was the sort of girl that acts of violence, which haunt the streets like ghosts on the lookout for a body they can fill, are deeply drawn to. She had last been seen going into Jacko's with a boy on a bike. Which boy? He was found – it was the bike that gave him away – but never publicly identified, though we all knew his name. He admitted he and Valmay had been in there. They had both come out. But Valmay stayed missing. They combed Jacko's inch by inch and found no trace of her, though some of the searchers found things they, or others, had lost there and had spent years looking for. It was a real treasure-trove that came out of the hunt for Valmay. You could have weighed her against the heap of it and the heap would have weighed more.

They dug in places where the ground was disturbed, they dragged the river. Nothing.

Rumours flew about. She had been seen getting into a car – a Holden, or a Ford ute, or a Customline – poor little thing! It was her innocence now, suddenly restored, that people were drawn to. Then the news came back that she was in Sydney, in a Salvation Army Home, having a baby. One boy got a postcard from her. Several others spent anxious days in the weeks afterwards running out to waylay the postman in the fear that she might drop them a line as well. They are middle-aged now, my generation. One is our local baker, another a real-estate agent, another a circuit judge. Our lives these days barely cross. One of them does odd jobs out at the golf course and we exchange a few words now and then. Not about Valmay. Others I see driving their daughters to dances or calling for them afterwards, just as in the old days, or at football matches where their grandsons are playing.

Still, it's an older fellowship we share than the ones we belong to now, Rotary, or the Lions, or the BMA; and in a ghostly, dreamy area of ourselves, some of us are still willing to acknowledge it. The gangs we ran with back there, whose passionate loyalties did not last – the scratch teams for rounders, with captains choosing in turn. You can look about, if you have an eye for these things, at a public meeting where people are vociferously taking sides, or round the spectators at a concert, or in the thin gathering at an Anzac Day service, and re-form, in a ghostly way, those older groups, and see something that is oddly moving: darker loyalties, deeper affinities, submerged now under the more acceptable ones. The last luminous grains of a freer and more democratic spirit, that the husbands and wives of my generation still turn to in dreams. It's like having the power to see into someone's pocket, where among the small change and dustballs he is still turning over a favourite taw.

It is this, all this, that will go under the bars of neon lights and the crowded shelves and trolleys of the supermarket, the wheels of skateboards, the bitumen walks and solid, poured-concrete ramps.

Jacko's, as we knew it, will enter at last into what a century and more has already prepared it for, the dimension of the symbolic. Which is of course what it has always been, though the grit of it between your bare toes and the density of its undergrowth, the untidy mass of it against the evening sky, for a long time obscured the fact. After all, you don't lose something as palpable as a solid silver cigarette lighter, not to speak of your innocence, in a place that is purely symbolic. Or gash your foot there so that you carry for ever after the consequent scar. Or stand, day after day, waiting to be called as the possible ninth, the tenth man of a team, in an agony of humiliation you feel may never end.

So it will be gone and it won't be. Like everything else.

Under.

Where its darkness will never quite be dispelled, however many mushroom-lights they install in the parking lot.

Where it will go on pushing up under the concrete, reaching for the wilderness further out that its four and a half acres have always belonged to and which no documents of survey or deeds of ownership or council ordinances have ever had the power to cancel. The possibility of building over it was forestalled the moment it got inside us. As a code-word for something so intimate it can never be revealed, an area of experience, even if it is deeply forgotten, where we still move in groups together, and touch, and glow, and spring apart laughing at the electric spark. There has to be some place where that is possible.

If there is only one wild acre somewhere we will make that the place. If they take it away we will preserve it in our head. If there is no such place we will invent it. That's the way we are.

Lone Pine

DRIVING at speed along the narrow dirt highway, Harry Picton could have given no good reason for stopping where he did. There was a pine. Perhaps it was that – its deeper green and conical form among the scrub a reminder out here of the shapeliness and order of gardens, though this particular pine was of the native variety.

May was sleeping. For the past hour, held upright by her seatbelt, she had been nodding off and waking, then nodding off again like a comfortable baby. Harry was used to having her doze beside him. He liked to read at night, May did not. It made the car, which was heavy to handle because of the swaying behind of the caravan, as familiar almost as their double bed.

Driving up here was dreamlike. As the miles of empty country fell away with nothing to catch the eye, no other vehicle or sign of habitation, your head lightened and cleared itself – of thoughts, of images, of every wish or need. Clouds filled the windscreen. You floated.

The clouds up here were unreal. They swirled up so densely and towered to such an infinite and unmoving height that driving, even at a hundred Ks an hour, was like crawling along at the bottom of a tank.

A flash of grey and pink flared up out of a dip in the road. Harry jerked the wheel. Galahs! They might have escaped from a dozen backyard cages, but were common up here. They were after water. There must have been real water back there that he had taken for the usual mirage. Like reflections of the sky, which was pearly at this hour and flushed with coral, they clattered upwards and went streaming away behind.

'May,' he called. But before she was properly awake they were gone.

'Sorry, love,' she muttered. 'Was it something good?'

Still half-asleep, she reached into the glovebox for a packet of lollies, unwrapped one, passed it to him, then unwrapped another and popped it into her mouth. Almost immediately she was dozing again with the lolly in her jaw, its cherry colour seeping through into her dreams.

THEY were on a trip, the first real trip they had ever taken, the trip of their lives.

Back in Hawthorn they had a paper run. Seven days a week and twice on weekdays, Harry tossed the news over people's fences on to the clipped front lawns: gun battles in distant suburbs, raids on marijuana plantations, bank holdups, traffic accidents, baby bashings, the love lives of the stars.

He knew the neighbourhood – he had to: how to get around it by the quickest possible route. He had got that down to a fine art. Conquest of Space, it was called, just as covering it all twelve times a week in an hour and a quarter flat was the Fight against

Time. He had reckoned it up once. In twenty-seven years bar a few months he had made his round on ten thousand seven hundred occasions in twelve thousand man-hours, and done a distance of a hundred thousand miles. That is, ten times round Australia. Those were the figures.

But doing it that way, piecemeal, twice a day, gave you no idea of what the country really was: the distances, the darkness, the changes as you slipped across unmarked borders.

Birds that were exotic down south, like those galahs, were everywhere up here, starting up out of every tree. The highways were a way of life with their own population: hitch-hikers, truckies, itinerant fruit-pickers and other seasonal workers of no fixed address, bikies loaded up behind and wearing space helmets, families with all their belongings packed into a station wagon and a little girl in the back waving or sticking out her tongue, or a boy putting up two fingers in the shape of a gun and mouthing Bang, Bang, You're Dead, kids in panel-vans with a couple of surf-boards on the rack chasing the ultimate wave. Whole tribes that for one reason or another had never settled. Citizens of a city the size of Hobart or Newcastle that was always on the move. For three months (that was the plan), he and May had come out to join them.

Back in Hawthorn a young fellow and his wife were giving the paper run a go. For five weeks now, their home in Ballard Crescent had been locked up, empty, ghosting their presence with a lighting system installed by the best security firm in the state that turned the lights on in the kitchen, just as May did, regular as clockwork, at half-past five; then, an hour later, lit the lamp in their living-room and flicked on the TV; then turned the down-stairs lights off again at nine and a minute later lit the reading lamp (just the one) on Harry's side of the bed in the front bedroom upstairs.

Harry had spent a good while working out this pattern and had been surprised at how predictable their life was, what narrow limits they moved in. It hadn't seemed narrow. Now, recalling the smooth quilt of their bed and the reading lamp being turned on, then off again, by ghostly hands, he chuckled. It'd be more difficult to keep track of their movements up here.

There was no fixed programme – they took things as they came. They were explorers, each day pushing on into unknown country. No place existed till they reached it and decided to stop.

'Here we are, mother,' Harry would say, 'home sweet home. How does it look?' – and since it was seldom a place that was named on the map they invented their own names according to whatever little event or accident occurred that made it memorable – Out-of-Nescaf Creek, Lost Tin-opener, One Blanket Plains – and before they drove off again Harry would mark the place on their road map with a cross.

This particular spot, as it rose out of the dusk, had already named itself. Lone Pine it would be, unless something unexpected occurred.

'Wake up, mother,' he said as the engine cut. 'We're there.'

Two hours later they were sitting over the remains of their meal. The petrol lamp hissed, casting its light into the sur-rounding dark. A few moths barged and dithered. An animal, attracted by the light or the unaccustomed scent, had crept up to the edge of a difference they made in the immemorial tick and throb of things, and could be heard just yards off in the grass. No need to worry. There were no predators out here.

Harry was looking forward to his book. To transporting himself, for the umpteenth time, to Todgers, in the company of Cherry and Merry and Mr Pecksniff, and the abominable Jonas –

he had educated himself out of Dickens. May, busily scrubbing their plates in a minimum of water, was as usual telling something. He did not listen.

He had learned over the years to finish the Quick Crossword while half tuned in to her running talk, or to do his orders without making a single blue. It was like having the wireless on, a comfortable noise that brought you bits and pieces of news. In May's case, mostly of women's complaints. She knew an inordinate number of women who had found lumps in their breast and gone under the knife, or lost kiddies, or had their husbands go off with younger women. For some reason she felt impelled to lay at his feet these victims of life's grim injustice, or of men's unpredictable cruelty, as if, for all his mildness, he too were one of the guilty. As, in her new vision of things, he was. They all were.

Three years ago she had discovered, or rediscovered, the church – not her old one, but a church of a newer and more personal sort – and had been trying ever since to bring Harry in.

She gave him her own version of confessions she had heard people make of the most amazing sins and of miraculous conversions and cures. She grieved over the prospect of their having, on the last day, to go different ways, the sheep's path or the goat's. She evoked in terms that distressed him a Lord Jesus who seemed to stand on pretty much the same terms in her life as their cats, Peach and Snowy, or her friends from the Temple, Eadie and Mrs McVie, except that she saw Him, Harry felt, as a secret child now grown to difficult manhood that she had never told him about and who sat between them, invisible but demanding, at every meal.

Harry, who would have defended her garrulous piety against all comers, regarded it himself as a blessed shame. She was a good woman spoiled.

Now, when she started up again, he vanished into himself, and while she chattered on in the background, slipped quietly away. Down the back steps to his veggies, to be on his own for a bit. To feel in his hands the special crumbliness and moisture of the soil down there and watch, as at a show, the antics of the lighting system in their empty house, ghosting their lives to fool burglars who might not be fooled.

HARRY woke. His years on the paper run had made him a light sleeper. But with no traffic sounds to give the clue, no night-trains passing, you lost track. When he looked at his watch it was just eleven.

He got up, meaning to slip outside and take a leak. But when he set his hand to the doorknob, with the uncanniness of a dream-happening, it turned of its own accord.

The young fellow who stood on the step was as startled as Harry was.

In all that emptiness, with not a house for a hundred miles in any direction and in the dead of night, they had come at the same moment to opposite sides of the caravan door: Harry from sleep, this youth in the open shirt from— but Harry couldn't imagine where he had sprung from. They faced one another like sleepers whose dreams had crossed, and the youth, to cover his amazement, said 'Hi' and gave a nervous giggle.

He was blond, with the beginnings of a beard. Below him in the dark was a woman with a baby. She was rocking it in a way that struck Harry as odd. She looked impatient. At her side was a boy of ten or so, sucking his thumb.

'What is it?' Harry asked, keeping his voice low so as not to wake May. 'Are you lost?'

He had barely formulated the question, which was meant to fit this midnight occasion to a world that was normal, a late call by neighbours who were in trouble, when the young man showed his hand. It held a gun.

Still not convinced of the absolute reality of what was happening, Harry stepped back into the narrow space between their stove and the dwarf refrigerator, and in a moment they were all in there with him – the youth, the woman with the baby, the boy, whose loud-mouthed breathing was the only sound among them. Harry's chief concern still was that they should not wake May.

The gunman was a good-looking young fellow of maybe twenty. He wore boardshorts and a shirt with pineapples on a background that had once been red but showed threads now of a paler colour from too much washing. He was barefoot, but so scrubbed and clean that you could smell the soap on him under the fresh sweat. He was sweating.

The woman was older. She too was barefoot, but what you thought in her case was that she lacked shoes.

As for the ten-year-old, with his heavy lids and open-mouthed, asthmatic breathing, they must simply have found him some-where along the way. He resembled neither one of them and looked as if he had fallen straight off the moon. He clung to the woman's skirt, and was, Harry decided, either dog-tired or some sort of dill. He had his thumb in his mouth and his eyelids fluttered as if he was about to fall asleep on his feet.

'Hey,' the youth said, suddenly alert.

Down at the sleeping end, all pink and nylon-soft in her ruffles, May had sat bolt upright.

'Harry,' she said accusingly, 'what are you doing? Who are those people?'

'It's all right, love,' he told her.

'Harry,' she said again, only louder.

The youth gave his nervous giggle. 'All right,' he said, 'you can get outa there.'

Not yet clear about the situation, May looked at Harry.

'Do as he says,' Harry told her mildly.

Still tender from sleep, she began to grope for her glasses, and he felt a wave of odd affection for her. She had been preparing to give this young fellow a serve.

'You can leave those,' the youth told her. 'I said *leave 'em*! Are you deaf or what?'

She saw the gun then, and foggily, behind this brutal boy in the red shirt, the others, the woman with the baby.

'Harry,' she said breathlessly, 'who *are* these people?'

He took a step towards her. It was, he knew, her inability to see properly that most unnerved her. Looking past the man, which was a way also of denying the presence of the gun, she addressed the shadowy woman, but her voice had an edge to it. 'What is it?' she asked. 'Is your baby sick?'

The woman ignored her. Rocking the baby a little, she turned away and told the youth fiercely: 'Get it over with, will ya? Get 'em outa here.'

May, who had spoken as woman to woman, was deeply offended. But the woman's speaking up at last gave life to the boy.

'I'm hungry,' he whined into her skirt. 'Mummy? I'm hungreee!' His eye had caught the bowl of fruit on their fold-up table. 'I wanna banana!'

'Shuddup, Dale,' the woman told him, and put her elbow into his head.

'You can have a banana, dear,' May told him.

She turned to the one with the gun.

'Can he have a banana?'

The child looked up quickly, then grabbed.

'Say ta to the nice lady, Dale,' said the youth, in a voice rich with mockery.

But the boy, who really was simple-minded, lowered the banana, gaped a moment, and said sweetly: 'Thank you very much.'

The youth laughed outright.

'Now,' he said, and there was no more humour, 'get over here.'

He made way for them and they passed him while the woman and the boy, who was occupied with the peeling of his banana, passed behind. So now it was May and Harry who were squeezed in at the entrance end.

'Right,' the youth said. 'Now—' He was working up the energy in himself. He seemed afraid it might lapse. 'The car keys. Where are they?'

Harry felt a rush of hot anger.

Look, feller, he wanted to protest, I paid thirty-three thousand bucks for that car. You just fuck off. But May's hand touched his elbow, and instead he made a gesture towards the fruit bowl where the keys sat – now, why do we keep them there? – among the apples and oranges.

'Get 'em, Lou.'

The woman hitched the baby over her shoulder so that it stirred and burbled, and was just about to reach for the keys when she saw what the boy was up to and let out a cry. 'Hey you, Dale, leave that, you little bugger. I said leave it!'

She made a swipe at him, but the boy, who was more agile than he looked, ducked away under the youth's arm, crowing and waving a magazine.

'Fuck you, Dale,' the woman shouted after him.

In her plunge to cut him off she had woken the baby, which now began to squall, filling the constricted space of the caravan with screams.

'Shut it up, willya?' the youth told her. 'And you, Dale, belt up, or I'll clip y' one. Gimme that.' He made a grab for the magazine, but the boy held on. 'I said, give it to me!'

'No, Kenny, no, it's mine. I found it.'

They struggled, the man cursing, and at last he wrenched it away. The boy yowled, saying over and over with a deep sense of grievance: 'It's not fair, it's not fair, Kenny. I'm the one that found it. It's mine.'

Harry was flooded with shame. The youth, using the gun, was turning the pages of the thing.

'Someone left it in a café,' Harry explained weakly. 'Under a seat.'

The youth was incensed. He blazed with indignation. 'See this, Lou? See what the kid found?'

But the woman gave him only the briefest glance. She was preoccupied with the baby. Moving back and forth in the space between the bunks, she was rocking the child and sweet-talking it in the wordless, universal dialect, somewhere between syllabic spell-weaving and an archaic drone, that women fall into on such occasions and which sets them impressively apart. The others were hushed. May, lowering her voice to a whisper, said: 'Look here, if you're in some sort of trouble— I mean—' She indicated the gun. 'There's no need of that.'

But the youth had a second weapon now. 'You shut up,' he told her fiercely. 'Just you shut up. You're the ones who've got trouble. What about this, then?' and he shook the magazine at her.

She looked briefly, then away. She understood the youth's outrage because she shared it. When he held the thing out to her she shook her head, but he was implacable.

'I said, look!' he hissed.

Because of the woman's trouble with the baby he had lowered

his voice again, but the savagery of it was terrible. He brandished the thing in her face and Harry groaned.

'Is this the sort of thing you people are into?'

But the ten-year-old, excited now beyond all fear of chastisement, could no longer contain himself.

'I seen it,' he crowed.

'Shuddup, Dale.'

'I seen it . . .'

'I'll knock the bloody daylights out of you if you don't belt up!'

'A cunt, it's a cunt. Cunt, cunt, cunt!'

When the youth hit him he fell sideways, howling, and clutched his ear.

'There,' the youth said in a fury, swinging back to them, 'you see what you made me do? Come here, Dale, and stop whinging. Come on. Come on here.' But the boy had fled to his mother's skirts and was racked with sobs. The baby shrieked worse than ever. 'Jesus,' the youth shouted, 'you make me sick! Dale,' he said, 'come here, mate, I didn't mean it, eh? Come here.'

The boy met his eye and after a moment moved towards him, still sniffling. The youth put his hand on the back of the child's neck and drew him in. 'There,' he said. 'Now, you're not hurt, are you?' The boy, his thumb back in his mouth, leaned into him. The youth sighed.

'Look here,' May began. But before she could form another word the youth's arm shot out, an edge of metal struck her, and 'Oh God,' she said as she went down.

'That's enough out of you,' the youth was yelling. 'That's the last *you* get to say.'

She thought Harry was about to move, and she put out her hand to stop him. 'No, no,' she shouted, 'don't. It's all right – I'm all right.' The youth, in a kind of panic now, was pushing the gun into the soft of Harry's belly. May, on her knees, tasted salt, put her fingers to her mouth and felt blood.

'All right, now,' the youth was saying. He was calming himself, he calmed. But she could smell his sweat. 'You can get up now. We're going outside.'

She looked up then and saw that it made no difference that he was calm. That there was a baby here and that the mother was concerned to get it to sleep. Or that he was so clean-looking, and strict.

She got to her feet without help and went past him on her own legs, though wobbling a little, down the one step into the dark.

THE tropical night they had stepped into had a softness that struck Harry like a moment out of his boyhood.

There were stars. They were huge, and so close and heavy-looking that you wondered how they could hold themselves up.

It seemed so personal, this sky. He thought of stepping out as a kid to take a piss from the back verandah and as he sent his jet this way and that looking idly for Venus, or Aldebaran, or the Cross. I could do with a piss right now, he thought, I really need it. It's what I got up for.

They were like little mirrors up there. That's what he had sometimes thought as he came out in the winter dark to load up for his round. If you looked hard enough, every event that was being enacted over all this side of the earth, even the smallest, would be reflected there. Even this one, he thought.

He took May's hand and she clutched it hard. He felt her weight go soft against him.

The youth was urging them on over rough terrain towards a patch of darker scrub further in from the road. Sometimes behind them, but most often half-turned and waiting ahead, he could barely contain his impatience at their clumsiness as, heavy and tender-footed, they moved at a jolting pace over the stony ground. When May caught her nightie on a thorn and Harry tried to detach it, the youth made a hissing sound and came back and ripped it clear.

No words passed between them. Harry felt a terrible longing to have the youth speak again, say something. Words you could measure. You knew where they were tending. With silence you were in the open with no limits. But when the fellow stopped at last and turned and stood waiting for them to catch up, it wasn't a particular point in the silence that they had come to. A place thirty yards back might have done equally well, or thirty or a hundred yards further on. Harry saw with clarity that the distance the youth had been measuring had to do with his reluctance to get to the point, and was in himself.

The gun hung at the end of his arm. He seemed drained now of all energy.

'All right,' he said hoarsely, 'this'll do. Over here.'

It was May he was looking at.

'Yes,' he told her. 'You.'

Harry felt her let go of his hand then, as the youth had directed, but knew she had already parted from him minutes back, when she had begun, with her lips moving in silence, to pray. She took three steps to where the youth was standing, his face turned away now, and Harry stretched his hand out towards her.

'May,' he said, but only in his head.

It was the beginning of a sentence that if he embarked on it, and were to say all he wanted her to know and understand in justification of himself and of what he felt, would have no end. The long tale of his inadequacies. Of resolutions unkept, words unspoken, demands whose crudeness, he knew, had never been acceptable to her but which for him were one form of his love – the most urgent, the most difficult. Little phrases and formulae that were not entirely without meaning just because they were common and had been so often repeated.

She was kneeling now, her nightie rucked round her thighs. The youth leaned towards her. Very attentive, utterly concentrated. Her fingers touched the edge of his pineapple shirt.

Harry watched immobilized, and the wide-eyed, faraway look she cast back at him recalled something he had seen on television, a baby seal about to be clubbed. An agonized cry broke from his throat.

But she was already too far off. She shook her head, as if this were the separation she had all this time been warning him of. Then went back to *him*.

He leaned closer and for a moment they made a single figure. He whispered something to her that Harry, whose whole being strained towards it, could not catch.

The report was sharp, close, not loud.

'Mayyeee,' Harry cried again, out of a dumb, inconsolable grief that would last now for the rest of his life, and an infinite regret, not only for her but for all those women feeling for the lump in their breast, and the ones who had lost kiddies, and those who had never had them and for that boy sending his piss out in an exuberant stream into the dark, his eyes on Aldebaran, and for the last scene at Todgers, that unruly Eden, which he would never get back to now, and for his garden choked with weeds. He meant to hurl himself at the youth. But before he could do so was lifted clean off his feet by a force greater than anything he could ever have imagined, and rolled sideways among stones that after a moment cut hard into his cheek. They were a surprise, those stones. Usually he was careful about them. Bad for the mower.

He would have flung his arms out then to feel for her comfortable softness in the bed, but the distances were enormous and no fence in any direction.

Her name was still in his mouth. Warm, dark, filling it, flowing out.

THE youth stood. He was a swarming column. His feet had taken root in the earth.

Darkness was trembling away from the metal, which was hot and hung down from the end of his arm. The force it contained had flung these two bodies down at angles before him and was pulsing away in circles to the edges of the earth.

He tilted his head up. There were stars. Their living but dead light beat down and fell weakly upon him.

He looked towards the highway. The car. Behind it the caravan. Lou and the kids in a close group, waiting.

He felt too heavy to move. There was such a swarming in him. Every drop of blood in him was pressing against the surface of his skin – in his hands, his forearms with their gorged veins, his belly, the calves of his legs, his feet on the stony ground. Every drop of it holding him by force of gravity to where he stood, and might go on standing till dawn if he couldn't pull himself away. Yet he had no wish to step on past this moment, to move away from it into whatever was to come.

But the moment too was intolerable. If he allowed it to go on any longer he would be crushed.

He launched himself at the air and broke through into the next minute that was waiting to carry him on. Then turned to make sure that he wasn't still standing there on the spot.

He made quickly now for the car and the group his family made, dark and close, beside the taller darkness of the pine.

Blacksoil Country

⊚⊚

THIS is blacksoil country. Open, empty, crowded with ghosts, figures hidden away in the folds of it who are there, who are here, even if they are not visible and no one knows it but a few who look up suddenly into a blaze of sunlight and feel the hair crawl on their neck and know they are not the only ones. That they are being watched or tracked. They'll go on then with a sense for a moment that their body, as it goes, leaves no dent in the air.

Jordan my name is. Jordan McGivern. I am twelve years old. I can show you this country. I been in it long enough.

When we first come up here, Pa and Ma and Jamie and me, we were the first ones on this bit of land, other than the hut-keepers and young inexperienced stockmen that had stayed up here for a couple of seasons to establish a claim, squatting in a hut, running a few cattle, showing the blacks they'd come and intended to stay and had best not be interfered with.

When we come it was to settle. To manage and work a run of a thousand acres, unfenced and not marked out save on a map that wouldn't have covered more than a square handkerchief of it and could show nothing of what it was. How black the soil, how coarse and green the grass and stunted the scrub and how easy a mob can get lost in it. Or how the heat lies over it like a throbbing cloud all summer, and how the blacks are hidden away in it, ghosts that in those days were still visible and could stop you in your tracks.

Mr McIvor, who owned the run, had no thought of coming up here himself. He was too comfortable out at Double Bay, him and his wife and two boys in boots and collars that I saw when I went out with Pa to get our instructions. I talked to them a bit, and the older one asked me if I could fight, but only asked; he didn't want to try it. This was in a garden down a set of wooden steps to the water, with a green lawn and a hammock, and lilies on green stalks as long as gun barrels, red.

Mr McIvor meant to stay put till the land up here was secured and settled and made safe. He might come up then and build a homestead. Meantime, my pa was to be superintendent, with a wage of not much more than a roof over our heads and a box of provisions that come up every six months by bullock dray, eleven days from the coast. To hold on to the place and run the mob he had stocked it with.

Our nearest neighbours were twelve miles off, southwest, and had blacks to work for them out of a mob that had settled on the creek below their hut. We only heard of this, not seen it. We had just ourselves. Pa believed it was better that way, we relied on nobody but ourselves. It was the way he liked it. Ourselves and no other. He wouldn't have slept easy with blacks in a mob close by, in a camp and settled. Maybe wandering in and out of the yards, or the hut even, and sleeping close by at night. Or not sleeping.

'You trust nobody, boy, there's nobody'll look out for you

better'n yourself. I learned that the hard way. I'm learnin' it to you the easy way, if you'll listen. We're on our own out here. That's the best way to be. No one watchin', or complainin' about this or that you done wrong, or askin' you to do it their ways. Just us. We're on to a good thing this time. We'll make it work. Damn me if we won't!'

There had been other places, a good many of them, where it didn't work. He had no luck, Pa. After a time there was always some trouble. There was something in the work he was asked to do, or the way the feller asked it, got his goat, and irked or offended him. He'd begin to walk round with that set, ill-used look to him that you knew after a time to avoid, and I would hear him, low and sulky, complaining to Ma after they had gone to bed. You could hear the aggrievement in his voice and the stubbornness and pride in his justifications.

I don't know when I first begun to see he wasn't always in the right. I might have picked it up in the first instance from Ma, from her silence, or from the way she'd start packing up her bits and pieces, things she had had from way back before I was born – a tea caddy made of tin with little pigtailed Chinamen on it, a good-sized greenish stone from the Isle of Skye, which is where she was from – them and whatever else she had an affection for and had saved out of our many wrecks. She had already begun to pack them up in her head before he even come out with it, that we were on the move again.

'I won't be treated like a bloody nigger,' he'd be telling her. 'A man's got a right to a bit of respect.' I don't know how many times I heard him say that, and saw the fierce look he wore, and felt the air hiss out of him and saw the scared look in her eye.

It was his pride. His impatience, too. Something in him that made doing things another man's way impossible to him.

I never once heard him put it down to anything he had done himself, to the trouble he had knuckling under or settling. It was always someone else was to blame. Or some power of bad luck or malice against him that all his life had dogged and downgraded him, going right back, and which he saw in the many forms it took to bring him low. In a look on one feller's face that said: 'This work is not done the way I want it. It is not to my liking. Do it again. An' if you can't do it my way, then we'd better part company.' Or in a finger moving slowly up a column of figures, and a frown that said: 'Hello, what's this?' Then that cloud of old hurt and misjustice on his face for being once again doubted and disrespected, and while he raged and justified, the bundling up, all in a rush, of our few bits of things.

Always the same end to every venture, no matter how hopeful he started out: anger and disappointment. But what I saw on those occasions was more than disappointment. It was shame. In front of Ma, and of me too I think, once he begun to consider me. At having so little power to hold us in one place and safe. At being always at the mercy of another man's discontents.

He wasn't always right. But Ma did not once, that I ever heard, cross him or argue back. We stuck together. We were loyal. If I learned that, it was not so much from what he told me of the necessity of it, which he did often enough, but from watching her.

Whatever strung the different places together was in what she made. In the first meal we ate there, the plates set out the same way as at the last meal we'd sat down to, and a bit later the line of clothes she'd have drying, with the wind of the new place lifting and puffing them full of sunlight. In the smile she'd allow herself when he told her, with all his old false confidence: 'This is a good place, Ef – an' he's a good man, I reckon. This'll do us for a bit – what d'you say?'

But I'd noticed something else by then. That people somehow, where he was concerned, were not well-disposed, they were not kindly. He lacked whatever it is that makes people respond.

Maybe he was just too much himself. Too ungiving. Or maybe

it was the opposite – he wasn't ready enough to receive. Anyway, he could never get it right, never manage to ask for a thing in a way that won men over. He'd ask and they'd frown and hum and shift their feet in the dirt, and he'd already have took offence or lost his temper before they'd even come up with an answer. They'd feel then that they'd been right to hold back, and him that he'd been a fool ever to ask.

He also discovered after a while, and long before I even knew what it was, that I did have it – the power, whatever it is, to soften people, win them over. He'd get me to ask for things he knew no amount of asking on his part could get him, and laugh up his sleeve at the way they'd been hooked. And even if it was a gift he despised and wouldn't have wanted for himself, he was happy enough for me to make use of it. He'd just stand there and listen while I soft-soaped them, and I could tell from the way he looked and smiled to himself, but it was a sour smile, that he scorned me. He was pleased I could do it, but it was something in me that he scorned and might come to hate in the long run – that's what I thought. He didn't know how I'd got hold of it, where it had come from. Not from him, not from his blood. So I needed all the more to stick close and show him, whatever he thought, that there was a connection. That I was loyal, blood-loyal, and always would be, come whatever. Whatever.

I T was blacksoil country, and when the rains come, all mud. The land flowed then like a river as wide as the horizon in all directions. In the dry it was baked hard, and cracked. The low scrub got so green that the light of it hurt your eyes, and when the grass sprung up it was a lawn for two or three days, like Mr McIvor's lawn out at Double Bay, then it was swaying round your knees and next thing you knew the cattle were lost in it. He cursed it and had a complaint about every aspect of it. Most of all about the blacks, as if all the faults of the country were their doing. As if they'd made it the way it was.

'They'd better keep clear a' this place, that's all I got to say,' he'd tell people. Our neighbours the Jolleys, for instance, the one or two times we met.

'Oh, the blacks are all right if you treat 'em right,' Mick Jolley would say.

'Yair,' he'd say, 'well, my idea of treatin' 'em right is to keep 'em where they bloody belong. Which is not on my property. Not while I'm in charge of it.' And he spat, and wiped the sweat off his face with a red handkerchief he wore, and screwed his eyes up against the glare of green.

Fact is, I loved this place we'd come to. Better than any other we'd been in.

He didn't. Not really. Nor Ma neither. For her it was a kind of horror, I knew that, though she would never have admitted it.

It was further out than we'd been before, and for her it was too far. All the things that tied her to the world – a store where she could turn things over at a counter, even if she couldn't afford to buy, a bit of material or that to pass through her fingers, a bit of talk, the sight of other women and what they were wearing – a new style of bonnet or the cut of a pair of shoes. All that, and the comfort of neighbours, of being linked that way, was gone. She went out only to hang the wash on the line, and even then I don't believe she ever raised her eyes to the country. She just acted as if it wasn't there.

But I loved it.

This is my sort of country, I thought, the minute I first laid eyes on it. And the more I explored out into it the more I felt it was made for me and just set there, waiting.

It was more than it looked. You had to give it a chance to show itself. There were things in it you had to get up close to, if you were to see what they really were – down on your knees, then sprawled out flat with your chest and your kneecaps touching it, feeling its grit. Then you could see it, and smell the richness of it too, that only come to your nostrils otherwise after a good fall of rain, when the smells were in the steam that rose up for just seconds and were gone.

Most of all I liked the voices of it. The day voices, magpies and crows and the rattle of cicadas, and the night voices, spotted nightjars calling caw-caw-caw gabble-gabble-gabble, and owls, and frogs I had never seen by day but heard after dark, so I knew they must be there, and found them at last, so small it was no wonder I'd missed them, and with the trick of taking on the colour, green or stripy-bark-like, of whatever they were clamped to, and only their eyes catching the light like tiny dewdrops, liquid and gleaming, till they blinked.

Nothing in it scared me. Not even the tiger snakes or diamond-heads you saw basking in the sun, then slithering off between hissing stems.

After a bit I would get up nights, let myself out and lie in some place out there under the stars. Letting the sounds rise up all around me in the heat, and letting a breeze touch me, if there was one, so I felt the touch of it on my bare skin like hands.

KEEPING the blacks off the land was a difficult proposition. Little groups of them – women and children dawdling along and chatting as they dug with sticks, bands of fellers on a hunting party – were forever straying across what we knew were our rightful boundaries.

Pa would put up with it for a bit, then go out with a gun and shout at them. There would be scowls and mutterings, and a shaking of spears on their side if it was the men, and on our side Pa, standing square and hard-mouthed, showing no fear, whatever he might have felt, with his shotgun across his arm.

He didn't have to point it. It was enough that he had it across his arm. They knew by now what it could do.

They were noisy and fierce-looking, them fellers, but it was show; and so on Pa's side was the shotgun. Only our show was more convincing, I reckon. Our noise, if it come to that, would be a single blast. Louder than anything they could produce, and they knew it. Louder, and from a darker place than a mere mouth.

I think Pa liked what it felt like to just stand there and watch them fellers dance and shout, singing out loud enough, but powerless. It made him all the quieter, just standing and watching how the puff went out of them after a bit. One or two of the fiercer ones among them would make a run, but only two or three steps, and he'd stand his ground, smiling to himself, no need to react.

It was a feeble token. They'd already decided to back off. And when they did, slinking off one by one and throwing dark looks over their shoulder, and muttering, he'd keep standing. I think it was the best he ever got to feel maybe in his life, being left like that facing the empty bush, the last one in the field.

If it was a bunch of just women and little kids he didn't even bother to confront them. He'd just fire the shotgun once in the air, and laugh at the way they squealed and run about rounding up their kids, then scattered.

Most of the time I was there beside him, since most of the work to be done round the place we did together. I was his off-sider, his chief helper. We had no others.

I was too half-grown and scrawny to offer him much physical support, but me being not yet a grown man, even by their lights, was a constraint on them, and in that I gave him an advantage he didn't maybe appreciate. I know this because when I didn't have any jobs to do for Ma, and wasn't out working with him, I'd wander off alone and pass right close to them and all they'd do, whatever they were engaged in, was look. They never offered any word of threat. They'd just look. Like I was some curious creature that had come into view, that was of no use to them because I couldn't be hunted, and was just there – but in a way maybe that changed things and made them curious.

They didn't give me any acknowledgment, either one way or the other, except just with their long looks.

And no trouble, neither. But I'd feel the skin creep on my skull, and I'd walk on as if I was walking on eggshells or air, and I'd just whisper to Jamie, if he was with me, 'Just keep on walkin', Jamie, and don't give 'em no notice,' and felt there was a kind of magic around us, that come from their looking and protected us from harm. Though all it might be was us being so young.

And that day?

It seemed no different from any of the other occasions. We were in the home paddock grubbing out the last of a patch of low mulga scrub, him all strained and sweating with a rope around his middle, me with a crowbar under the dug-out roots. Suddenly he looked over my head and said quietly: 'Get me gun, Jordie. Leave that now.'

I looked to where he was looking and didn't move quick enough for him. He had slipped clear of the rope. He jerked his elbow at me and I jumped and run. When I come back he was standing with an odd little smile on his face. I don't think I'd ever seen him so good-humoured, so playful-looking.

Before he took the gun from me he rubbed his palms on the side of his pants; they were grimed with dirt and sweat from the rope. Then, still smiling a little, he ran his fingers through his hair.

He had curls that sometimes flopped into his eyes. Now, with his fingers, he smoothed them back and his bronze-coloured hair was dark wet.

I handed him the gun and he kept watching while he loaded it. He had never taken his eyes off them. But what I remember, even more than what was happening, was the mood that was on him. That was what was unusual. The rest was like any other occasion. He shot me a lively look that said, 'Watch this now, Jordie,' as if what was coming was to be the purest fun. I loved him at that moment. He was so easy. So happy-looking.

The blacks, all near naked, were striding along through the scrubby dust and in the heat-haze seemed to bounce on their heels and rise up a little. To float.

There were three of them. The leading one carried something slung across his shoulders; they weren't near enough yet for us to see what it was. And there was a small mob at their back, not many. A dozen, no more. About thirty yards back, in the scrub.

There was no way we could have known what it was. We'd had no notice they were coming.

Pa put his hand up to stop them. They kept coming at the same slow pace, their bodies swaying a little, or so it looked, as if they were walking on air. 'Stop there,' he shouted. They were closer than they had ever got before.

'That's far enough,' he called. They were still coming.

I looked across to him then. He was all fired up, but not panicky. Not angry neither, but he had a brightness to him I had never seen before. It was like I could hear the blood beating in him, or maybe it was mine. I think it was the moment in his life, so long as I had ever known him, when he felt lightest, most sure of himself, most free. Five minutes back he'd been straining his guts out over that stump, every muscle of him strained – the sweat running out of him in streams. He was still sweating now, but it was a glow.

He raised the gun and I thought: 'He'll just fire over their heads and scare them.' He fired, and I saw the black, the leading one, take off into the air a little and what he was carrying on his shoulders fly up. And as he stumbled in mid-air and rolled towards us, the meat, the side of lamb, went rolling in front of him. Meantime, the other two were scurrying back, and the mob gave a cry, and the women begun wailing. It was done. It had happened.

Out of that slow-fired mood he was in. Which did not ebb away. So that even when he saw what he had done, and lowered the gun, he was still lightly smiling.

I was astonished. That he could stand there with the sound of the shot still in the air and all that yelling and be so cool. Inside the heat there had been a cold, clear place, and he had acted from there, lightly and without thought. It was like he had just hit on a new way of being inside his own skin, and from now on that was the way he would live, and I was the first, the very first, to get a glimpse of it. But he wasn't thinking of me. He just turned his back on the whole thing, and swaggering a little, walked away, leaving the blacks, who were quiet now, to creep forward and drag off the man who had been killed or wounded, while the side of meat just lay where it was, rolled in the dirt.

Later on I saw that it must have seemed like a good idea on Mick Jolley's part to send the blacks across like that. To show him, Pa, that they could be trusted. That he could just send them off like that with a gift and it would be delivered. Sort of a soft lesson to him. But how was he to know that that was what it was? All in a moment and with no warning. A mob of blacks just walking up where he had always resisted.

He was wrong, I know that. He was wrong every way. But I want to speak up for him too.

Even when Mick Jolley come across and yelled at him and tried to get him to pay the blacks what he called compensation, I was on his side; not just by standing there beside him, but in my heart.

He did not know that black was a messenger. Who had the

right to pass through all territories without harm. How could he know that? And even if he had, he mightn't have cared anyway that it was a consideration in their world. It wasn't one in ours. That they should even have considerations – that there might be rules and laws hidden away in what was just makeshift savagery, hand-to-mouth getting from one day to the next and one place to another a little further on over the horizon – that would have seemed ridiculous to him. Given they had no place of settlement nor roof over their heads to keep the sun off, nor walls to keep out the wind and the black dust that made another duller black- ness where they were already blacker than the most starless night. No clothes neither, to keep them decent, and had never raised even the skinniest runt of a bean or turnip, nor turned a single clod to grow what went into their mouths, only scavenged what was there for anyone to crawl about and pick up. 'Consideration,' he would have said. 'Consideration, thunder!'

Yet it was true. There were messengers. Given a part to play like any sergeant or magistrate, and recognized as such even by strangers.

Though not by us.

Which made us, in some ways, the most strangers of all.

I don't believe he knew what he had done – the full extent of it. And with all that light in his blood that made him so glowing and reckless, I don't think he would have cared.

I didn't know neither, but I felt it. A change. That change in him had changed me as well and all of us. He had removed us from protection. He had put us outside the rules, which all along, though he didn't see it that way, had been their rules. The magic I'd felt when they just stood and looked, as if I was some creature like a unicorn maybe, had come from them. Now it was lifted.

These last months I had taken to going about the place with Jamie. I was just beginning to show him things, things I had

discovered and knew about our bit of land that no one else did
except maybe the blacks, and places no one else had ever been
into, except maybe them, when it was theirs. I don't reckon those
hut-keepers and shepherds had ever been there. They were places
you could only reach by letting yourself slide down a bank into a
gully or pushing in under the low underbrush along a creek, so
low you had to go on your knees, then on your belly. Jamie
would have followed me anywhere, I knew that, but I was careful
always to show him marks and signs along the way. Even when
he was too little to talk, he was quick to see, and knew the signs
again on the way back. He had known no other place than this.
There were times, little as he was, when I felt he was showing it
to me. Only now I kept a good eye open when we were out
together. The whole country had a new light over it. I had to look
at it in a new way. What I saw in it now was hiding-places. Places
where they were hidden in it, the blacks. Places too where ghosts
might be, also hidden.

THE story I have been telling up till now is my story. But at this
point it becomes his. Pa's.

It is the story of a twelve-year-old boy treacherously struck
down in the bush by unknown hands, his body hidden away in the
heart of the country and for days not found, though many search-
parties go looking.

The mother is distraught. She has only one woman to comfort
her. All the rest of those who gather at the hut, take a hasty
breakfast and set out in small groups to scour the countryside, are
men, embarrassed to a profound silence by the depth of her grief.
Only when they have stepped into the sunlight again, to where
their horses stand restless in the sun, do they let their breath out
and express what they feel in head-shaking, then anxious whispers.

They feel a kind of shyness in the presence of the father as well, but there are forms for what they can say to him. They clap him roughly on the shoulder, and impressed by the rage he is filled with, which they see as the proper form for his grief, they reach for words that will equal his in their stern commitment, their vehemence.

He is a man who has been touched by fate, endowed with the dignity of outrage and a cause. It draws together, in a tight knot, qualities that they felt till now were scattered in him and not reliable. When the body comes to light at last, the skull caved in, the chest and thighs bearing the wound-marks of spears, and he rides half-maddened about the country urging them to ride with him and kill every black they come across, he inspires in them such a mixture of horror and pity that they feel they too have been lifted out of the ordinary business of clearing scrub and rounding up cattle and are called to be heroic.

He is a figure now. That is why it is his story. The whole country is his, to rage up and down in with the appeal of his grief. His brow like thunder, his blue eyes bleared with weeping, he speaks low (he has no need to shout) of blood, of the dark pull of it, of its voice calling from the ground and from all the hidden places of the country, for the land to be cleared at last of the shadow of blood. He is a new man. He has discovered one of the ways at last to win other men to him and he blazes with the power it brings him. He is monstrous. And because he believes so completely in what he must do, is so filled with the righteous ferocity of it, others too are convinced. They are drawn to him as to a leader.

One clear cool act, the shedding of a little blood, and all that old history of slights and humiliations, of being ignored and knocked back, of having to knuckle under and be subservient — all that is cancelled out in the light he sees at last in other men's eyes, in their being so visibly in awe of the distinction that has descended upon him.

But that little blood was my blood, not just that black feller's. Pa's blood too. So he did come to see at last that I was connected.

For a season my name was on everyone's lips, most of all on his, and in the newspapers at Maitland and Moreton Bay and beyond. Jordan McGivern. A name to whip up fear and justified rage and the unbridled savagery of slaughter. For a season.

The blacks in every direction are hunted and go to ground. They too have lost their protection – what little they had of it. And me all that while lying quiet in the heart of the country, slowly sinking into the ancientness of it, making it mine, grain by grain blending my white grains with its many black ones. And Ma, now, at the line, with the blood beating in her throat, and his shirts, where she has just pegged them out, beginning to swell with the breeze, resting her chin on a wet sheet and raising her eyes to the land and gazing off into the brimming heart of it.

Great Day

☺☺

I

UP at the house, Angie told herself, they would be turning in their bunks and pushing off sheets in the growing heat, still dozing but already with their sights on breakfast. Bacon and eggs and Madge's burnt toast. 'Burnt?' Madge would bluster; 'I don't call that burnt, I can do better than that. Besides, burnt toast never did your father any harm. It didn't kill him off, he thrived on it, so did your uncles. Now, who's for honey and who wants Vegemite? That's the choice.' The children would yowl and make faces but bite into the burnt toast just the same. It was a ritual that would begin precisely at seven with the banging of Madge's spoon.

Meanwhile, down here on the headland, in an expanding stillness in which clocks, voices and every form of consciousness had still to come into existence and the day as yet, like the sea, had no mark upon it, it was before breakfast, before waking, before everything but the new tide washing in over rows of black, shark-toothed rocks that leaned all the way inland, as they had done since that moment, unimaginable ages ago, when the earth at this point whelmed, gulped and for the time being settled. Angie drew her knees up and locked them in with her arms.

On the reef to her left, out of sight behind the headland, her father-in-law, Audley, was fishing.

Dressed in the black suit and tie he wore on all occasions, even before breakfast, even for fishing, and standing far out on the rocky ledge with its urchin pools and ropes of amber worry-beads, he would, she thought, if you were sailing away and happened to glance back, be the last you would see of the place, a sombre column – or if you were coming from the other direction, the first of the natives, providing, with his fishing rod and jacket formally buttoned, an odd welcoming party.

She raised her eyes to the sea and let herself drift for a moment in its dazzling stillness, then, dawdling a little, got to her feet and started up the path towards the house.

A FOUR-SQUARE structure of sandstone blocks, very massive and permanent-looking, it stood immediately above the sea. Its first builder was Audley's grandfather. Successive owners had simply added on in the style of the times: two bedrooms on the south in Federation shingles; later, for the children, the product of wartime austerity, a fibro sleepout. More recently Audley had added a deck of the best kauri pine where in winter they could eat out, protected at last from the prevailing southerlies, and where, when the whole clan was gathered, the overflow, as Madge called it, could bed down in sleeping-bags. The grass below the deck was scythed – no mower could have dealt with it – and roses, mixed with native shrubs, threw out long sprays forming an enclosure that was alive at this time of day with wrens and long-beaked honey-eaters. Angie, lifting aside a thorny shoot, came round past the water tank. She paddled one foot, then the other, in the bucket of salt water Madge had set below the verandah and came round to the kitchen door.

'Hey, here's Angie.'

Her son, Ned, leapt up among the scattered crusts.

'Angie,' he shouted as if she were still fifty yards off, 'did you know Fran was coming?'

'Yes,' she said, 'Clem's bringing her.'

Ned was disappointed. He loved to be the bearer of news.

Always ill at ease in Madge's kitchen, fearful she might register visible disapproval of the mess or throw out some bit of rubbish that her mother-in-law was specially keeping, Angie perched on the end of a form as in a class she was late for and accepted a mug of scalding tea.

'But I thought they were divorced,' Ned protested. His voice cracked with the vehemence of it. 'Aren't they?'

Madge huffed. 'Drink your tea,' she told him.

'But aren't they?'

'Yes, you know they are,' Angie said quietly, 'but they're still friends. I saw Audley,' she added, to change the subject.

Jenny looked up briefly – 'Has he caught anything?' – then back to the album where she was pasting action shots of her favourite footballers. She was a wiry child of nine, her hair cut in raw, page-boy fashion. Angie cut it for her.

'The usual, I should think,' said Madge. 'A cold.'

'I thought when people got divorced,' Ned persisted, 'it was because they hated one another. Why did they get divorced if they're still friends? I don't understand.'

Jenny, who was two years younger, drew her mouth down, looked at her mother, and rolled her eyes.

'Ned,' Angie said, 'why don't you go and see if Ralph's up?'

'He is, I've already seen him,' Jenny informed her. Ralph was their father. 'He's writing. He told me to stay away.'

'People never tell me anything,' Ned exploded. 'How am I ever going to know how to act or anything if I can't find out the simplest thing? How will I—'

'You'll find out,' Madge said. 'Now – I want a whole lot of wild spinach to make soup. I'm paying fifty cents a load. Any takers? A load is two bucketfuls.'

'Oh, all right,' Ned agreed, 'I'll do it, but fifty cents is what you paid last time. Haven't you heard of inflation?'

'Ned,' Madge told him firmly, 'it's too early in the morning for an economics lecture. Besides, you know what a dumb-cluck I am. Leave me in blessed ignorance, that's my plea.' She made a clown's face and both children laughed. 'Small hope in this family!'

When she had armed the children with short knives and buckets she flopped into a chair and said: 'Do you think we'll get through today? I'm a dishrag already and it isn't even eight.'

THE Tylers were what people called a clan. Not just a family with the usual loose affinities, but a close-knit tribe that for all its insistence on the sociabilities was hedged against intruders. Girls brought home by one or another of the four boys would despair of ever getting a hold on the jokes, the quick-footed allusions to books, old saws, obscure facts and references back to previous mealtimes that made up a good deal of their table-talk, or of adapting to Madge's bluntness or Audley's sombre, half-joking pronouncements, the latter delivered, in the silence that fell the moment he began to speak, in a voice so subdued that you thought you must have been temporarily deafened by the previous din.

Even when they had been gathered in as daughters-in-law, they felt so out of it at times that they would huddle in subversive pockets, finding relief in hilarity or in whispered resentment of the way their husbands, the moment they crossed the family threshold, became boys again, reverting to forms of behaviour that Madge, in her careless way, had allowed and which Audley, for all his fastidiousness, had been unable to check: shouting one another down, banging with their great fists, grabbing at the food or scattering it to left and right in a barbarous way that in minutes left any table they came to a baronial wreck.

Audley claimed descent from two colonial worthies, a magistrate and a flogging parson, both well recorded. His roots were as deep in the place as they could reasonably go. Madge, on the other hand, had no family at all.

Adopted and brought up by farm people, she had been, when Audley first knew her, in the days when they came down here only for holidays, the Groundley girl, who helped her old man deliver milk.

'Goodness knows where you kids spring from,' she used to tell the boys when they were little. 'Only don't go thinking you might be princes. Just as well Audley knows what little sprigs of colonial piety and perfect breeding you are because there's nothing I can tell you. Gypsies, maybe. Tinkers. Malays. Clem could be a Malay, couldn't you, my pet? Take your pick.'

'I was fascinated, you see,' Audley would put it, taking people aside as if offering a deep confidence. 'I'd been hearing all my life about my lot – the Tylers and the Woolseys and the Clayton Jones – it made me feel like something in a dog show. Then Madge came along with those blue eyes and big hands that belonged to no one but herself – old Groundley was a little nut of a fellow. In our family everything could be traced back. Long noses, weak chests, a taste for awful Victorian hymns – it could all be shot home to some uncle or aunt, or to a cousin's cousin that only the aunt had heard of. My God, I thought, is there no way out of this? Whereas I can look at one of the boys and say, Now I wonder where he got that from? Can't be my side, must be her lot. The berserkers. The Goths-and-Vandals. It's made life very interesting.'

People who were not used to this sort of thing were embarrassed. But it was true, the boys all took after their mother, except for Clem, who took after no one. They were big-boned, fair-headed, with no physical grace but an abundance of energy and rough good humour. Not a trace of Audley's angular refinement, though they were free as well of his glooms.

As little lads Madge had let them run wild, go unwashed, barely fed – in the upper echelons of the public service where Audley moved it was a kind of scandal – but had been ready at any time to down tools and read them a story or show them how to spin pyjama cord on a cotton-reel or turn milkbottle-tops into bells. She wrote children's books, tall tales for nine-year-olds. Twice a year, regardless of household moves or daily chaos or childhood fevers or spills, she had produced a new title – she was proud of that – using as models first her children, then her grandchildren, all thinly disguised under such names as Bam or Duff or Fizzer for the boys and for the tomboyish girls, McGregor or Moo. 'It's lucky,' she told Ned and Jenny once, 'that Audley had all those family names to draw on. I'd have let my fancy rove. If it'd been up to me I'd have called the boys all sorts of things.'

'What would you have called Ralph?' Ned asked, interested in catching his father for a moment in a new light.

'I'd have called him – let me see now – Biffer!'

The children went into volleys of giggles. 'That's a great name!' Ned yelled; 'it really fits him. You should have called him that.'

'I did,' Madge said, 'in one of my books, I forget which.'

'I know,' Jenny shouted, '*The Really-Truly Bush*, I've read it. The boy in that was Biffer.'

'Well, hark at the child, she got it in one.' Madge gave a snort of laughter.

But Ned was affronted. 'That's not Ralph,' he insisted; 'that's nothing like him. That's not Ralph.'

'No,' Madge agreed, 'but that's because a whole lot of different things happened to that boy. If they'd happened to Ralph he'd be just like it.'

'Would he really?' This from Jenny.

Ned, whose idea of the world was very different, was unconvinced.

Madge laughed again. 'Really and truly.'

She got letters from her readers which she answered in the same distracted style as the books and had been looked up to by three generations of children as the mother they most wished for, a cross between a mad aunt and a benign but careless witch.

The boys too had had no complaint, though they had from the beginning to give up all hope of shirts with all the buttons on or matching pyjama tops or even a decently cooked potato. It was Audley who had attended to them, wiping their noses, picking up their toys, dishing up Welsh Rarebit, which he had learned to make at cadet camp when he was a schoolboy and which had remained his only culinary skill. They had had to fend for themselves, shouting one another down in the war for attention and growing up loud and confident. They admired their mother without qualification and were fond of Audley as well – too much so, some would have said. 'The true sign of a great soul,' they would have replied, citing Goethe, 'is that it takes joy in the greatness of others.' They were quoting their father, of course.

Today was to be a meeting of the clan. All the Tylers would be there with their wives and children, a few cousins, and neighbours from as far as fifty kilometres off if they cared to drive over.

It was the Tylers' annual party, an occasion they celebrated as a purely family affair since it was Audley's birthday. That it coincided with a larger occasion was of only minor significance – though Audley, when he was a boy, had thought it might not be, and had built his dreams on the auspicious conjunction. Later, when some of those dreams became reality, he mocked his youthful presumption as tommy-rot, but by then it had already served its purpose.

'No, no, Audley's seventy-second,' Madge was shouting into the phone. 'Just come along as usual if you've got nothing better on, it won't be special. Oh no, Audley's birthday, like we always do. The other thing's too big. I couldn't cater.'

WHEN Audley came up the path he did have something: two blackfish, each the size of an Indian club.

'Oh la,' Madge said, 'now what am I going to do with those?' She stood with her hefty arms folded, looking down at where he had laid them side by side on the bench, the eyes in their heads alive but stilled, a pulse still beating under the gills. 'The freezer's full of things for the party. Isn't he the last word?'

Audley, meanwhile, in his jacket and tie and with his long legs crossed, was perched on a form, hoeing into tea and burnt toast.

Angie watched him. He chewed on the blackened wafer as if he were doing penance. He appeared to enjoy it. He wants people to think he's humble, she thought.

She could never quite believe, despite the evidence, that in Audley she had come so close to power. He had none of the qualities you read about in books, but for thirty-seven years this odd, hunched figure, who was devoting himself at the moment to ingesting the last of a blackened crust, had been in charge, one after the other, of four government departments. Wasn't that power? His signature had appeared on the nation's banknotes. He had, as he put it, 'had tea with the sharks', survived a dozen blood-lettings, dealt with thugs of every political persuasion. Six prime ministers at one time or another had slipped into his office, sometimes with a bottle of whisky, to steel their nerves before a vote or share a moment's triumph or grief, and still turned up, those of them who were among the living, to check a detail in their memoirs or clear up with him a matter of protocol or just talk over what was happening in the world – meaning Canberra.

He had disciples too. The oldest among them now ran departments of their own or were professors or the editors of journals. The youngest were alert, ambitious fellows who saw in him the proof that you could get to the top, and stay there too, yet maintain a kind of decency. He bit into the blackened crust, masticating slowly, while Madge, arms folded, regarded the fish.

'Well,' she said at last, 'this won't buy the baby a new blanket. Birthday or no birthday, I've got my words to do.'

She hefted the two fish into the sink, scratched about on the windowsill among the biros, testing one or two of them to see if they were still active, then, using her forearms to push back a pile of plates, made space for herself at the table among the unwashed tea mugs. She opened a child's plastic-covered exercise book and began to write.

Angie wandered off. She ought by now to be used to Madge's off-hand discourtesies and Audley's tendency to withdraw, but the truth was that she always felt, down here, like a child who had been dumped on them for a wet weekend and could find nothing to do.

She went down the steps and stood shading her eyes, looking to where the children would be hunting the slopes above the sea for spinach. Suddenly, as if from nowhere, an arm came round her waist, so awkwardly that they nearly went over, both of them, into a blackberry bush.

'Hullo,' Ralph said, 'it's me. Are you up to a bit of no good?' He kissed her roughly on the side of the neck. 'Hope no one's looking.' He kissed her again.

He was a big fair fellow who had never grown out of the schoolboy stage of being all arms and legs, a bluff, shy man who liked to fool about, but then, without warning, would go quiet, as if his intelligence had just caught up with some other, less developed side of him that was all antics, leaving him suddenly abashed.

He pulled her down in the grass.

'Mmm,' he mumbled into her mouth, 'this is better than Mum's toast.' He sat up. 'Did Dad catch anything?'

She told him about the blackfish and he nodded his head, suddenly sober again.

'Oh, he'll be pleased with that, that's good,' he said. 'What a terrific day it's going to be.'

II

AN hour later Jenny was shouting from the verandah rails. 'Hey Ned, Mum, Fran's here.' She ran down to the gravel turning-place to greet her.

'Where's Clem?' she demanded when she saw that Fran was alone. 'Angie said you were coming with Clem.'

Fran stuck her head out of the window to look behind and backed into a shady place under the trees.

'We came in separate cars,' she explained. 'He's closing the gates.'

Almost immediately they heard his engine on the slope.

Fran swung out of the car carrying the little deerskin slippers she liked to wear when she was driving, coral pink, and a soft leather shoulder bag. She was very slight and straight, and with her cropped hair looked childlike, girlish or boyish it was hard to say.

'So,' she demanded, glancing about, 'what have you kids been up to?'

'When?'

'Since I last saw you, dope!' She gave Ned's head an affectionate shove, then threw her arm around him. She was barely the taller.

He grinned and hunched into himself but did not pull away.

'Our football team won the premiership,' Jenny announced. 'I got best and fairest.'

'Gee,' said Fran, 'did you?'

Clem slammed the door of his car and came up beside her. Smiling, he took her hand. 'Do we look like newlyweds?' he asked.

Jenny was suddenly suspicious. 'Why?' she asked. 'Why should you?'

'I don't know. Do we?'

The two children glanced away.

Since his accident Clem *said things*, just whatever came into his head. They felt some impropriety now and cast quick glances at Fran to see what she thought of it, but she didn't appear to have heard. 'I'm going to look for Angie,' she said jauntily. 'I could do with a cuppa.' She started off towards the house with her bouncy, flat-heeled stride. With the long scar across his brow, Clem was smiling.

At the step to the verandah Fran had turned and was waiting for him.

One night three years back, on a straight stretch between a patch of forest and the Waruna causeway, a child had leapt out suddenly on to the moonlit gravel. It was late, after ten. Clem was tired after a long drive. The boy, who was nine or ten years old, was playing chicken. He stood in the glare of the headlights, poised, ready to run, while his companions – who were all from the Camp, half a dozen skinny seven- or eight-year-olds – danced about on the sidelines yelling encouragement, and the little girls among them shrieked and covered their eyes.

Clem swung the wheel, narrowly avoiding the boy, and the whole continent – the whole three million square miles of rock, tree-trunks, sand, fences, cities – came bursting through the windscreen into his skull. The remaining hours of the night had lasted for fourteen months. It had taken another year to locate the bit of him that retained the habit of speech.

Always the odd man out among them, the stocky dark one, he was a good-natured fellow, cheerful unless taunted, but slow, tongue-tied, aimless. Even at thirty he had been unable to see what sort of life he was to lead. It was as if something in him had understood that no decision was really required of him. The accident up ahead would settle that side of things.

When Fran first came to the house it was with one of the others. She had been Jonathon's girl. But in time the very qualities that had impressed her in Jonathon, the assurance he had of being so much cleverer than others, his sense of his own power and charm, appeared gross. They got on her nerves in a house where everyone was clever, and shouted and pushed for room.

An outsider herself, never quite sure that Madge approved of her and whether to Audley she was anything more than an angry mouse, she had seen Clem as a fellow sufferer among them and decided it was her role to save him. From Them. She would take him away, where he could shine with his own light. 'There, you see,' she wanted to tell them, 'you have been harbouring a prince among you.'

'You're making a grave mistake,' Madge warned her once while they were in the kitchen washing up.

'Oh?' she had replied, furiously drying. 'Am I?'

The marriage lasted two years.

After being at passionate cross-purposes for a year, they lived a cat and dog life for another, each struggling for supremacy, then separated. But when Fran got back from her year in Greece they had begun to see one another again, locked in an odd dependency. She was adventurous, what she wanted was experience, 'affairs'. Clem was the element in her life that was stable. And after his accident, she became the one person with whom he felt entirely whole.

'So,' she demanded now, 'what do they say about me turning up like this?' 'They' meant Madge and Audley.

She had her bare feet up on a chair, a straw hat over her eyes. She looked, Angie thought, wonderfully stylish and free.

'Nothing. They wouldn't say anything to me.'

'Huh!'

Fran pushed the hat back, screwed her nose up and squinted against the glare off the sea.

They were friends. When Fran first appeared all those years ago – Angie was already a young wife, Fran then just another of the hangers-on – they had been wary of one another; they were so unalike.

She thinks I'm bossy, like them, Fran had told herself. A know-all. A skite.

She thinks, Angie had thought, that I'm a dope.

But then they became sisters-in-law and found common cause. Angie, with Fran to lead her, discovered how much stronger her resentments were now that she had someone to share them. She admired Fran's fierce sense of humour, was bemused by her assumption that being honest gave her the right to be cruel. Fran, when she wearied, as she often did, of her own intensity, was drawn to Angie's stillness, her capacity to just sit among all that Tyler ebullience and remain self-contained.

When they were alone together Fran made a game of her rage, doing imitations of Audley's voice and manner and little turns of phrase that kept them in a state of exhausted hilarity. But Angie could never quite free herself of a feeling of discomfort, of something like impiety, when Fran took her flair for mockery too far.

The fact was that for all his peculiarities, Audley was without doubt the most remarkable person she had ever known. On this point she agreed with Ralph. Then, too, there was something in him, a side of his odd, contradictory nature, that Fran had no feeling for and for which she had coined the nickname 'Doctor Creeps'. But it was just this quality in him that Angie felt most connected to, since she recognized in it something of herself. When Fran mocked it she felt the opening between them of a dispiriting gap, a failure of sympathy on Fran's part that must include herself as well.

Angie's darkness was inherited. The Depression was already a decade past when she was born, but she had grown up with it just the same. In her parents' house it had never ended; they were still waiting for the axe to fall. She had married to break free of that cramped and fearful world and had been surprised, when her father-in-law engaged her with a sorrowful look that said, Ah, *we* know, don't we, that even among the Tylers there was this pocket of the darkly familiar.

Audley had ways of disguising his moodiness with bitter jokes and a form of politeness that at times had an edge of the murderous. 'Your glass is empty,' he would say to some unsuspecting guest, leaning close and whispering, full of hospitable concern, and Angie would shudder and turn away.

'So,' Fran said, 'what's the cast list at this wake? As if I didn't know! Jonathon, Rupe and Di, the Rainbow Serpent—'

Angie laughed.

'God, why did I come? Am I really such a masochist? Well, you'd better not answer that.'

Clem, meanwhile, was with his mother at the pinewood bench in the house, sipping tea from a chipped mug while she chopped and prepared spinach. Madge looked up briefly, then away. The scar across his brow was so marked that all other signs of age seemed smoothed away in him.

'Tell me when I was six, Mum,' he was saying, and he gave a cheery laugh as at an old joke between them. Madge paused, then chopped.

It was a thing he used to say when he was a little lad of nine or so: 'Tell me when I was six,' he would say, 'when I was four, when I was just born.' It was an obsession with him. But no detail you gave was ever enough to convince him that he really belonged among them.

Madge had had no time for the game then. Too many other questions to answer. And the house, and their homework, and Audley's many visitors. Now she made time. Clem's questions were the same ones he had been asking for nearly thirty years, but these days they had a different edge. Ashamed to reveal how much of his life was a blank, he had become skilful at trapping others into providing the facts he was after. Starting up a conversation or argument with Audley and his brothers, he would turn his head eagerly from one to another of them like a child catching at clues that the grown-ups would give away only by default; or he would begin stories that the others, with their passion for exactitude, would immediately leap to correct.

'You should ask Audley,' Madge told him now, turning her eyes from his glowing face. 'He's the archive.'

'But I want *you* to tell me.'

She paused, looked at the worn handle of her knife. 'You were a strange little lad,' she began after a moment.

He laughed. 'How was I strange?'

'You had this knitted beanie you liked to wear.'

'What colour?'

'Red. It was a snow cap, in fact, though we never went near the snow. It looked like a tea-cosy. It was too big for you, but you wouldn't go anywhere without it. It made you look like a sort of mad elf. If I said no, you'd rage at me.'

'What would I say?'

'I can't remember what you'd say. Just the look of you.'

'Was this when I was six?'

'Five, six, something like that.'

'Go on.'

'Ralph used to refuse to go out with you. My God, what a pair you were! People will look, he'd tell me, they'll think he's a dill.'

'Was I?'

'No, of course you weren't. You were just a funny little boy.' She paused and looked at him. 'Don't you remember any of this, Clem?'

'No,' he said happily. 'It's all news to me.'

He wasn't a dill. He had, in fact, been an intense, old-fashioned little fellow, but with a form of intelligence that wasn't quick like the others – a sign, perhaps, an early one, of a relationship to the world that was to be obscure and difficult and a life that was not to shoot forward in a straight line but would move by missteps and indirections through all those crazes taken up and dropped again that had filled a cupboard with abandoned roller-skates, a saxophone, a microscope and slides, all the gear for scuba diving.

He looked down now, embarrassed by what he had to ask, but hitched his shoulders and plunged in.

'Did you and Dad love me?'

His voice was painfully urgent, but what struck her, as she clutched the knife to her breast, was his odd, dislocated cheerfulness. She closed her eyes.

There were times, years back, when they were all shouting and clutching at her skirt, when she would, for just a second, close her eyes like this and pretend they were not there, that they had succumbed to lockjaw or whooping-cough, or had never found the way through her to their voices and demanding little fists. It was restful. She could rest in the emptiness of herself, but only for a second. Immediately struck with guilt, she would catch up the littlest of them and smother him with kisses, till he felt the excessiveness of it and fought her off.

'What's it like,' some silly young woman had once asked her, one of the hangers-on, 'to live in a house full of boys?'

She had given one of her straight answers: 'The lavatory seat is always up.'

Now, opening her eyes again, she looked at Clem, at the darkness of his brow, and said, 'Of course we did. Do. How could we help it?' He stared at her with his blue eyes, so clear that they could see right through you. 'You were Audley's favourite – always. You know that. If he was hard on you sometimes it was because he was afraid of his own feelings, you know how he is. Of being swept away.'

'I thought I was a disappointment to him.'

'Maybe. Maybe that too. Things get mixed up. Nothing's just one thing. You know that.'

He nodded, fixing his eyes on her, very intent, an alert seven-year-old, as if there was something more to what she was saying than the words themselves expressed, some secret about Life, the way the world is, that he would some day catch and make use of.

'Ah, here's your father,' she said, relieved at the promise of rescue. Audley was coming up the track between the banksias.

Clem immediately leapt to his feet. Hurling himself through the wire-screen door and down the steps, he flung his arms around his father, clasping him so tight that Audley, with his head thrown back and his arms immobilized, had the look of a black-suited peg-doll. 'Clem,' he said, clutching at his glasses, but allowing himself to be danced about as Clem hung on and shouted: 'It's me, Dad, I'm so glad to see you!'

III

M OSEYING about on the slope beyond the house in swimming trunks, sneakers and a green tennis-shade, Ned glimpsed through the trees a party of interlopers. Stopped on the stony track, among blackboys and leopard gums that had been blackened the summer before by a bushfire, they were gathered in a half-circle round a charred stump.

Slipping from tree to tree like a native, Ned began to stalk them. There were six adults and some children.

The men, who were young, wore jeans and T-shirts, except for one with hair longer than the others and tied with a sweatband, who wore a singlet and had tattoos. They carried sleeping bags, an esky, and the man with the tattoos had a ghetto-blaster. Two of the women carried babies.

Ned manoeuvred himself into a better position to see what it was that had stopped them.

An echidna, startled by their footfalls on the track, had turned in towards the foot of the stump and, with its spines raised, was burrowing into the ashes and soft earth, showing a challenge, but pretending, since it could not see them, that it was invisible.

'What is it?' one of the women was asking.

'Porcupine,' one of the men told her, and the man with the tattoos corrected him: 'Echidna'.

'Gary, come away,' the other woman said, and she hauled out a boy of five or six who was dressed as a space invader and carried a plastic ray-gun.

Ned, very quietly, squatted, took a handful of ashes and smeared them over his cheeks, forehead and neck, then took another and smeared his chest.

If I was really a native, he thought, and had a spear, I could drive them off. They don't even know I'm here.

It pleased him that while they had their eyes on the echidna, which was only pretending to be invisible, he had his eye on them and really was invisible, camouflaged with earth and ashes and moving from one to another of the grey and grey-black trunks like a spirit of the place. He was filled with the superior sense of belonging here, of knowing every rock and stump on this hillside as if they were parts of his own body. These others were tourists.

They were on their way to the beach. You could not legally stop them – the land along the shore was public, it belonged to everyone – but this headland and the next as well belonged to Audley and would one day be Ralph's, then his. He felt proprietorial, but responsible too. As soon as the party had moved on, he went and checked on the echidna, which was still burrowing. When he stepped out on to the track again he was surprised to find the space invader there, a sturdy, dark-headed kid with freckles.

'Hi,' the boy said cheerfully. 'We're gunna have a bonfire, you can come if you like. My name's Gary, I'm six.'

Ned was furious. It hurt his pride that he had been crept up on and surprised. He was disarmed for a moment by the boy's friendliness and lack of guile, but affronted by his presumption. It wasn't his place to offer invitations here.

The boy meanwhile was regarding him with a frown. 'You know what?' he said at last, 'you've got stuff all over your face.'

'I know,' Ned told him sharply, 'I don't need you to tell me,' and he began to walk away. The space invader followed.

'Don't go,' he shouted, as Ned, arms stiffly at his side, his body pitched forward at an odd, old-mannish angle, began to stride away downhill. 'We got sausages. D'you like sausages? We got plenty.'

Ned walked faster.

'We got watermelon, we got cherry cheesecake. Hey, boy,' he shouted, 'don't go away. My name's Gary, I already told you. What's yours?'

He was trotting after Ned on his plump little legs. 'Hey,' he panted, when he finally caught up, 'why are we walking so fast?'

Ned swivelled. 'You piss off,' he said from a height.

The boy looked at him as if he might be about to burst into tears, and when Ned turned and started off again, did not follow.

'Ralph!' Ned shouted as soon as he was in sight of the house, 'there's a whole heap of people up there going to make a bonfire. Can they?'

Ralph, hearing the note of hysteria in his voice, was tempted to laugh, but Ned was quick to take offence and Ralph was touched, as he often was, by the boy's intense concern about things. He was always in a blaze about something – the Americans in Nicaragua, what the Libs were up to in the Senate. Keeping his own voice even, he said: 'Well, it's a free country, Ned. They can have a bonfire if they want. So long as they're careful.'

Ned huffed. He had hoped his father might be more passionate. 'Well, I'm going to tell Audley,' he announced. He stalked off.

Audley was on the phone in the sitting-room. All morning he had been receiving congratulatory messages, most of them from people who would later be at the party. He stood hunched and with his head bowed, murmuring politenesses into the mouth-piece while, with his eyes screwed up in acute distress, he did a little stamping dance on the carpet and tugged with his free hand at a button on his vest.

Ned waited impatiently; then, when the call went on longer than he had expected, sprawled in an armchair and took up a magazine. At last Audley replaced the receiver. He stood a moment, looking gravely down. Ned, who was still all eagerness and anger, held back.

He was impressed by this grandfather of his, and not only by his reputation; also by the sense he gave, with his deep reserve, of being worthy of it.

Audley was on all occasions formal. Ned liked that. He had a hunger for order that the circumstances of his life frustrated. He wished that Angie and Ralph, whom he otherwise approved of in every way, would insist a little more on the rules. He would have liked to call Ralph 'sir', as kids did on TV. But everything around them was very free and easy – maybe because Ralph, when he was younger, had been a hippie.

'How are you, Ned?' Audley said at last, but went on standing, deep in thought. He might have been out in a paddock some-where, having got there, Ned thought, without even noticing, on one of his walks.

'Audley,' he began, very quietly, but Audley was startled just the same.

'Ah,' he said, 'Ned!'

Ned went on bravely: 'Do you know there are people on the headland? They want to make a bonfire.'

He watched for Audley's reaction, which did not come, and

was surprised how the urgency had gone out of the question, not just out of his voice, which he lowered out of consideration for Audley, but out of what he felt. He had taken on, without being aware of it, some of Audley's subdued gravity.

Audley seemed not to have heard the question. Putting his hand on Ned's head in a gentle, affectionate way, he stood looking down at the boy. 'So what do you think of today, eh, Ned?'

Ned was confused. He knew what Audley thought because it was what Ralph thought as well. They were to be non-participants in the national celebrations. 'Not wet-blankets,' Ralph had insisted. 'If these fellers want an excuse for a good do, I'm not the one to deny them, but it's just another day like any other really, when we've got to get along with one another and keep an eye on the shop.'

It was a view that did not appeal to Ned. It was unheroic. He would, if it could be done with honour, have gone out and waved a flag. He wanted time to have precise turning-points that could be marked and remembered.

'Well,' Audley said now, and turned aside. Ned slumped in his chair. Dissatisfied on that question as on the one he himself had put.

This is how it always is, he raged to himself. They like things left up in the air. They never want anything settled.

LATER that morning, and again in the afternoon, he went back to the headland to see what those people were up to.

The first time, the four men, stripped to their bathers, were playing football on the wet beach, making long rugby passes and shouting, tackling, scuffing up sand.

Three of them were hefty fellows with thickened shoulders and thighs. The fourth, the long-haired one who had previously worn a singlet, was slimmer and fast. They were all very white as if they never saw the sun, except that the slim one with the tattoos had a work-tan on his neck and arms that made him look as if he was still wearing the singlet, only now it was cleaner.

The boy was down at the shoreline dragging a wet stick. The two women, lying head to toe opposite one another in the shade, were waving off flies from the babies, who were asleep. They were talking, and every now and then one of them gave a throaty laugh. Ned sat for a long time watching.

When he went back the second time the men were dressed and their hair was wet. They had been surfing and were busy now constructing a bonfire, shouting to one another across great stretches of air and energetically competing to see who could drag out the longest branch and heave it crosswise on to the pile. They laughed a lot and every second word was 'fuck'.

The two women, each with a child on her hip, were walking along the edge of the tide, almost in silhouette at this hour against the wet sand, which was lit with rays of sunlight that shot out from under the clouds. Oyster-catchers were running away fast from their feet.

Once again he sat for a long time and watched. He wondered how high the bonfire would go before the men tired of hauling dead trees and brush out of the sandhills, and how far, once it was alight, it would be visible out at sea. He admitted now that what he really regretted was that the bonfire was not theirs. It ought to be theirs. The idea of a bonfire on every beach and the whole map of Australia outlined with fire was powerfully exciting to him. The image of it blazed in his head.

He got up and began to walk away, and almost immediately stumbled on the boy, who had been squatting on the slope behind him.

'Hi,' Ned said briskly, and walked on – a kind of reconcilement. It was too late for anything more.

IV

UNDER the influence of his birthday mood, which was sober but good-humoured, and in honour as well of the larger occasion, Audley decided on a walk to town.

He often took such a walk in the afternoon. It helped him think. He could, while strolling along, turn over in his mind the headings of a report he had to write, or prepare one of the speeches that since his retirement were his chief contribution to public life, polishing and repolishing as he walked phrases that would appear on the late-night news bulletins, to be mulled over the morning after by politicians, economists, friends, rivals and his successors in the various public-service departments he had once had at his command. It was an old trick, this recovery of the harmony between walking pace, our natural andante as he liked to call it, and the rhythms of the mind. 'I think best with my kneecaps,' he would tell young reporters, who looked puzzled but scribbled it down just the same. 'I recommend it.'

If he didn't feel like walking back he could get a boy from the garage to drive him or there was always some local, a farmer with his wife and kids or a tradesman with a ute full of barbed wire or paint tins, who would offer him a lift. He was a familiar figure in these parts, traipsing along with his head down, his boots scuffing the dust.

His object was not, as gossip sometimes suggested, the Waruna pub, though he did sometimes drop in there for an hour or so to hear what the locals had to say, but the museum just beyond, the Waruna Folk and History Museum as it was rather grandly called, which was housed in a four-roomed workman's cottage next to the defunct bank.

It had been founded by his grandfather in the early thirties, with furniture and other knick-knacks from the house and a rare collection of moths and beetles.

Other families over the years had added their own cast-offs and unfashionable bric-a-brac: superannuated washboards and mangles, butter-churns, a hip-bath, tools, toys, photographs. Holiday-makers on their way to the beach resorts further south would stop off to stretch their legs among its familiar but surprising exhibits. It was educational. They would point to a pair of curling-tongs or a shaving-dish that looked as if someone had taken a good-sized bite out of it, a ginger-beer bottle with a glass stopper, a furball as big as a fist that had been found in the stomach of a cat.

But the main body of the collection had come from the Tylers, so that stepping into the dark little rooms where everything was so cramped and crowded was for Audley like re-entering one of the abandoned spaces of his childhood, which had miraculously survived or been resurrected, but with different dimensions now and with all its furnishings rearranged.

The cedar table and twelve dining chairs, for example, that filled the front room, had once stood in the larger dining-room at the house, whose windows looked down to the sea, and when Audley seated himself – as he liked to do, though a notice expressly forbade it – in one of the stiff-backed carvers by the wall, and gazed out across the glazed table-top, he was disconcerted, startled even, when that view failed to materialize. He could not imagine mealtimes at this table in any other light.

He recalled such occasions vividly. The big people seated round the extended cedar table, he and the other children – his brother, various cousins – at side-tables by the wall.

The table, minus its extensions, was set now with dinner-plates from some other household and just the sort of engraved glasses that his grandmother, who was a snob, would have relegated to the back of a cupboard. He could imagine the well-dressed ghosts coming in through the door (and one or two of them, uncles, through the windows) and seating themselves in their accustomed places, a bit surprised by some of the details, as if one of the long string of maids his grandmother found and then let go had made an error, but happy just the same to find themselves back, and taking up immediately the never-ending arguments his grandmother wished they would refrain from – 'Not at the table, Gerry, please!' – and which as a boy he had longed to join.

Above the table hung a lamp. It was of an old-fashioned kind that was all the rage again, in coloured glass. He remembered climbing on to his father's shoulders to light it, and from that height seeing the room, as the flame took, spring into a new shape. It had looked foreshortened from up there, as if he had been seeing it as it was now, nearly seventy years later.

What he had failed to notice, on that occasion, was the old fellow in the suit seated on a chair against the wall.

His father's contribution to the museum was a collection of rock specimens and rare fossils, set out now in display-cases in the hallway, each piece labelled in neat copperplate, his father's hand, and the ink so faded it could barely be read. The shell fossils were of exquisite engineering, little spiral staircases in perfect section, the ferns indelible prints.

He had loved these objects as a child. As a young fellow of sixteen or seventeen he had often come here with his father to examine them and been led so deep by his awed contemplation of their age, and all his father had to tell, that he had thought that his fate, his duty, was to become a geologist and solve the mysteries of their land.

They still moved him, these dusty objects, but that particular fate had never been taken up, though it still hovered in his excited imagination, as if the dedication of his life to stones and minerals were still an option of his secretly enduring youth. Would the distinguished geologist he might have become – he had no doubt of the distinction – have been all that different? He doubted it.

Other people saw him, he knew, as if what he was now had been fixed and inevitable, a matter of character. He wished sometimes that he could introduce them to some of his favourites among those other lives he had been drawn to and had abandoned or let go. Like the jazz pianist who, for two or three summers, along with a saxophonist and drummer, had rattled round the countryside in an old Ford, using his left hand to vamp while he reached with the other for a glass – already on the way to an established drunkenness and sore-headed despair that he actually felt on occasion. As if that other self had never quite been dismissed. The museum was full of such loose threads that if he touched them would jerk and lead him back.

On a wall of the little ex-bedroom out the back were three photographs. One of them was of a class from the one-teacher school where he and old Tommy Molloy, the head-man out at the Camp, had started school together more than sixty years ago, singing the alphabet and their times-tables together at the same desk. If he poked his head out the window he could see the little verandahed schoolhouse under a pepper tree, in the grounds now of Waruna High.

The photograph had been taken two years before he and Tommy arrived there, in his brother Ralph's year.

He studied the faces. Sitting cross-legged in the front row, holding a slate on which Miss Curry, whose first name was Esme, had chalked Waruna One Teacher School, 1922, was Tommy's sister Lorraine.

She had been the best fisherman among them: that is what Audley recalled. Once, when the trevally were running, she had caught forty-three at a single go. The sea had been so thick with them that you could have walked on their backs from one side of the cove to the other, and he believed sometimes that they had done just that. It was one of the great occasions of his life.

Lorraine had gone off a year later to be a domestic somewhere. Her eyes in the photograph looked right through you. So alive and black you might think they were beyond defeat. Well, time had known better.

He set his fingertip to the glass – also forbidden, of course. The print it left was a mist of infinitesimal ghostly drops that in a moment faded without trace.

But it was something other than this old photograph, however moving he found it, that drew him to this room. In a display of children's toys – a jigsaw puzzle that some local handyman had cut with a fine jigsaw, a pipe for blowing bubbles, some articulated animals from a Noah's Ark – was a set of knucklebones. He had won them more than sixty years ago from a boy called Arden Robinson who, the year he was nine, had come to stay with neighbours for the Christmas holidays and for whom he had formed an affection that for five whole weeks had kept him in eager and painful expectation.

He had not meant to win. He had meant to give the knucklebones up as a token of the softness he felt, the lapse in him of the belief that he was the only one in the world who mattered. As a hostage to what he had already begun to think of as The Future. A sacrifice flung down to nameless but powerful gods.

But he had won after all. The holidays came to an end, he had never seen Arden Robinson again. He had kept the knucklebones by him as a reminder, then five years ago had given them over, his bones as he called them, into public custody, which was in some ways the most hidden, the most private place of all. It would be nice, he sometimes thought, if he could give himself as well.

Occasionally, sitting in a chair in one of the rooms, he would doze off, and had woken once to find a little girl preparing to poke a finger into him as if, propped up there in his old-fashioned collar and tie, he was a particularly convincing model of ancient, outmoded man. When he jerked awake and blinked at her she had screamed.

'I'd quite enjoy it, I think,' he told them at home, 'if instead of shoving me into a hole somewhere you had me stuffed and sat there. No need for a card. No need for anyone to *know* it was me.'

V

A T half-past seven the first of the guests arrived. Jenny was the look-out. Hanging from one of the verandah posts, she could see headlamps swinging through the dusk and stopping at the first of their gates. Two cars. There would be two more gates to open and close before they reached the gravel slope.

She leapt down and darted into the house.

'Madge, Angie,' she called, 'they're on the way. Somebody's here.'

Madge, in shoes now and a frock that emphasized the width of her hips, was standing at the sink, contemplating the two fish she had earlier found a place for at the bottom of the fridge but had now taken out again to make room for her dips.

Her whole life, she felt, had been a matter of finding room. For unhappy children, stray cats, pieces of furniture passed on by distant aunts, unexpected arrivals at mealtimes, visitors who stayed too long talking to Audley and had to have beds made up for them on the lounge-room sofa, gifts she did not want and could find no use for but did not have the courage to throw out. Now these fish.

'They're almost here,' Jenny was shrieking.

Fortunately it was only her son Jonathon with one of his girls, though he did warn her that Lily Barnes was in the car behind.

'Oh Lord,' she said. 'Jenny, love, go and tell Audley Lily Barnes is here. Oh, and Jonathon.' Only then did she embrace her son.

She took the flowers he had brought and dumped them absent-mindedly into the sink. Then, not to appear rude, she turned and kissed his girl, in case she had been here before. All Jonathon's girls were of striking appearance – more appearance than reality, she had once quipped – but she could never tell one of them from the next.

'How is he?' Jonathon asked, taking a handful of nuts from one of the bowls she had laid out and tossing them, one by one, into his mouth. 'What's been going on? What have I missed?'

'Nothing,' she told him, moving the bowl out of his reach. 'You haven't missed a thing. Now, if you're hungry, Jonathon, I'll give you some soup. I thought you'd have eaten on the way.'

'We did. We had this terrific meal, didn't we, Susie? At Moreton.' He reached behind her and took another handful of nuts. But immediately there was the sound of Lily's voice and Audley's greeting her.

'Well,' said Madge, 'that's the end of that.'

She strode out to the stone verandah.

'Is she always like that?' the girl whispered to Jonathon.

He looked at her with his mouth full. 'Oh,' he said, 'I thought you'd been here before.'

'No,' she said, coldly, 'I have not.'

Lily Barnes was an old flame of Audley's – that was Madge's claim, though he always denied it.

'Lily Barnes,' he would say, 'is a remarkable woman, but she's more than I could have handled.'

'La, hark at the man!' Madge would tell the boys, who, when they were young, had been all ears for these interesting revelations. 'That means he thinks he can handle me.'

'Can you, Dad?' one of them would pipe up. 'Can you?'

When Lily Barnes and Audley were at university they had been rivals for various medals and scholarships, which she had mostly won. But after they left, Audley had gone on to high public office; Lily had been, over the years, private secretary to a string of ministers, admired, feared, warily consulted, but a shadowy presence, unknown outside a narrow circle. Then when she retired three years ago she had published a book that upstaged them all, Audley included, and had become a celebrity. At seventy she was very plain and petite, twisted now with arthritis but always very formally and finely dressed.

Madge, years ago, had dubbed her the Rainbow Serpent, partly because of her sharp tongue but also because of a passion she had for coloured silks. She had meant it unkindly then, but in the years since the name had come to have a benign, over-arching significance. It was an affectionate tribute.

She entered now wearing a russet-coloured skirt and a café-au-lait blouse, leaning as always on a stick, but making an impression, for all her crooked stance and diminutive size, of elegance and charm. She had with her a young fellow, the son of some people she knew, called Barney Shannon, who had been in trouble with drugs and was now employed to drive her about. Since he wanted to bring his surfboard and was also shifting house, they had come in his ute, the back of which was piled high with his futon, several bits of old iron from which he hoped to make lampstands, a fifties cocktail cabinet and his library of paperbacks, all in cartons and covered with a loose tarpaulin.

'Sorry, Madge,' she called, 'are we the first? It's Barney. He drives like a bat out of Hades. I think that ute of his may have cured my back by redistributing the vertebrae.' She looked about and gave one of her winning smiles. 'But how lovely to be here.'

A n hour later the room was full. Little noisy groups had formed, mostly of men, all vigorously arguing. Lily, moving from one group to another and leaning on her stick, would linger just long enough to shift the discussion sideways with a single interjection, then move on. She did not join the other women, young and old, who sat on the sidelines.

Fran had been hovering at the edge of these groups. She too moved from one to another of them, growing more and more irritated by what she heard and angrier with herself for having come.

She knew these people. They were the same relations and old friends and nervous hangers-on that she had been seeing for the past fifteen years, people for whom disagreement was the spice of any gathering. She felt out of place. Not because her opinions were all that different from theirs, but from temperament, and because, as everyone knew, she was a backslider. She had married one of them, been taken to the heart of the clan, then bolted. Well, that was their version. Drink in hand, looking sad-eyed and defenceless, but also spikily vigilant, she kept on the move.

Clem watched her from cover. He had mastered the art of pretending that his attention was elsewhere while all his movements about the room, along the verandah, past the open windows, had as their single object her appearance in a mirror or between the shifting heads.

He watched. Not to monitor or restrict her freedom but to

centre himself. Otherwise the occasion might have become chaotic. All that din of voices. All those faces, however familiar. The fear that someone without warning might open their mouth and expect an answer from him.

Once, briefly, she had come up beside him. Her head came only to his shoulder.

'Are you okay?'

'Yes,' he told her, 'I'm doing fine. What about you?'

She cast a fierce glance about the room. 'I'll survive.'

He loved this house. He had grown up on holidays here. It was where he could let go and be free. All its routines, from the dinning of Madge's early-morning spoon to the pieces Audley liked to play on the piano last thing at night, were fixed, known. Objects too.

He liked to run his fingertips along the edge of the coffee-table and feel the sand under its varnish. His brother Rupe had made that table at Woodwork when he was fifteen. Clem loved it. It was one of the objects he had clung to when he was floating out there in the absolute dark, finding his way back by clinging to anything, however unlikely, that came to hand. Rupe's table had played no special part in his life till then, but he had clung to it, it had shored him up, and squatted now, an ugly, four-legged angel, right there in the centre of the room, very solid and low to the ground, bearing glasses and a lumpy dish full of cashews. He would have knelt down and stroked it, except that he had learned to be wary of these sudden impulses of affection in himself, towards people as well as objects, that were not always welcome or understood.

He had moments of panic still when he looked up and had no idea where he had got to. It was important then that something should come floating by that he recognized and could fling his arms around. The house was full of such things. Rupe's table,

Audley's upright, the jamb of the verandah door where a dozen notches showed how inch by inch he and his brothers had grown up and out into the world – Ralph always the tallest. He had never caught up with Ralph.

And the books! Old leather-bound classics that their grandfather had collected, Fenimore Cooper and Stevenson and Kipling, and magazines no one would ever look at again, except maybe him; tomes on economics and the lives of the great, Beethoven and Metternich, and the children's books he had loved when he was little. *The Tale of the Tail of the Little Red Fox* one of them was called. It contained a question that had deeply puzzled him then, and still did: how many beans make five? It sounded simple but there was a trick in it, that's what he had always thought, which was intended to catch quick-thinkers and save slow ones. But from what?

He could move among these familiar things and feel easy. But when Fran was here the course he followed, the line he clung to, was determined by her. He liked the way she led him without knowing it, the form she gave to his turning this way and that, and how she held him while herself moving free.

S H E came to the edge of a group where Jonathon, his new girl leaning on his shoulder and pushing segments of sliced apple between her perfect teeth, was listening to a story Audley's cousin, Jack Wild, was telling. Jack Wild was a judge.

Most of the group had heard the story before and were waiting, carefully preparing their faces, for the punchline. Catching her eye, Jonathon gave her one of his bachelor winks.

They had a compact, she and Jonathon. They steered clear of each other on these family occasions, but meeting as they sometimes did on neutral ground, at openings or at one of the places in town where they liked to eat, could be sociable, even affectionate, for twenty minutes or so, teasing, reliving the times before Clem, before the wars, when they had been like brother and sister, best mates. He wasn't hostile to her or sternly unforgiving, like Rupe and Di.

She winked back, and saw with satisfaction that the girl had seen it. A little crease appeared between her perfect brows.

A moment later she had moved to another group and was half listening, half inattentively looking about, when she caught the eye of someone she had never seen before, a boy – man – who was lounging against the wall and observing her over the rim of his glass.

She looked down, then away, and almost immediately he came up to her.

He was called Cedric Pohl and rather pedantically, a bit too sure of himself she thought, spelled it out for her: P-O-H-L. He already knew who she was. Oh yes, she thought, I'll bet you do! He was an admirer of Audley's, but his time with the clan had been in one of her periods away. He had been away himself. He was just back from the States.

She listened, looking into her glass, wondering why he had picked her out and searching for something she could hold against him, and settled at last on his expensive haircut. Her mouth made a line of silent mockery.

Because, his gathered attention said, the powerful energy he was directing at her – because you looked so lost standing like that. Alone and with your eyes going everywhere.

He was attracted, she saw, by her desperation. It attracted people. Men, that is. They felt the need to relieve her of it. To bring her home, as only they could, to the land of deep content. She had been through all this before.

She lifted her chin in sceptical defiance, but had already caught the note of vibrancy, of quickening engagement in his voice that stirred something in her. Expectancy. Of the new, the possible. Hope, hope. And why not? Again, the excitement and mystery of a new man.

Moments later, she was outside, taking breaths of the clear night air. On the grass below the new deck, some young people, children mostly, were dancing. A single high-powered bulb cast its brightness upwards into the night, but so short a distance that it only made you aware how much further there was to go. The stars were so close in the clear night that she felt the coolness of them on her skin.

She had moved out here to get away from the feeling, suddenly, that too much might be happening too fast. Glass in hand, she looked down at the dancers.

Ned was there. So was Jen, along with three or four of their cousins, one of them a little lad of no more than five or six, Rupe and Di's youngest. They were moving barefoot to the ghetto-blaster's tatty disco, looking so comically serious as they rotated their hips and rolled their shoulders in a sexiness that was all imitation – of sinuosity in the girls, of swagger in even the tiniest boys – that she wanted to laugh.

Jen glanced up and waved. Fran raised her hand to wave back and was suddenly a little girl again at the lonely fence-rails, waving at a passing train.

She had always been an outsider here; in the clan, among these people who believed so deeply in their own rightness and goodwill. They had meant to pass those excellent qualities on to her, having them, they believed, in their gift. But for some reason she was resistant and had remained, even after her marriage, one of the hangers-on, one of those girls in lumpish skirts and T-shirts (though in fact she had never worn clothes like that, even at nineteen) who'd got hooked on the Tylers, not just on whichever one of the boys had first brought them in but on Audley's soft attentions, Madge's soups, the privilege of being allowed to do the drying-up after a meal, the illusion of belonging, however briefly, to the world of rare affinities and stern, unfettered views they represented. Girls, but young men too, odd, lonely, clever young people in search of their real family, were caught and spent years, their whole lives sometimes, waiting to be recognized at last as one of them.

She had told herself from the beginning that she could resist them, that she would not, in either sense, be taken in.

In the early days, on visits like this, she had spent half her time behind locked doors, sitting on the lowered lavatory seat or cross-legged on her bed, filling page after page of a Spirex notebook with evidence against them: the terrible food they ate, their tribal arrogance and exclusivity, the jokes, everything they stood for – all the things she had railed against in grim-jawed silence when she was forced to sit among them and which, as soon as she was alone, she let out in her flowing, copy-book hand in reports so wild in their comedy that she had to stuff her fist into her mouth so that they would not hear, gathered in solemn session out there, her outrageous laughter, and come bursting in to expose her as God's spy among them. At last, in an attempt to rid herself of all memory of her humiliations and secret triumphs, she had torn up every page of those notebooks and flushed them down the loo in a hotel in Singapore, on her way to Italy and a new life.

Remembering it now, she was tempted to laugh and free herself a second time, and was startled by Audley's appearance, out of nowhere it might have been, right beside her.

'Let me get you something,' he said very softly, relieving her of her glass. Setting his sorrowful eyes upon her he gave her one of those looks that said: We know, don't we? You and I.

Do we? she asked herself, and felt, once again, the old wish to succumb, then the old repulsion and the rising in her of a still unextinguished anger.

These cryptic utterances were a habit with him, part of his armoury of teasing enticements and withdrawals. They were intended, she had decided long ago, in their suggestion of a special intimacy, to puzzle, but also to intimidate.

'You don't understand him,' Clem would tell her; 'you're being unfair.' But the truth was, there was something phony in these tremendous statements. A challenge perhaps for you to call his bluff and unmask him. Crooked jokes.

He paused now and, after a silence that was calculated, she thought, to the last heartbeat, went off bearing her glass.

Once again she felt the need to escape. I'll find Angie, she thought. She'll get me out of this. The last thing she wanted now was to get caught in an exchange of soul-talk with Audley.

She saw Angie standing alone in a corner, in a dream as usual, wearing that dark, faraway look that kept people off. How beautiful she is, Fran thought.

She was in black – an old-fashioned dress that might have belonged to her mother, with long sleeves and a high neck that emphasized her tallness. Fran was about to push between shoulders towards her when she felt a hand at her skirt. It was Tommy Molloy's wife, Ellie.

'Hi, Fran,' she said. 'You lookin' good.'

'Hi, El,' Fran said, and, settling on the form beside her, stretched out her legs and sat a moment looking at her shoes.

'Wasser matter?' the older woman asked, but humorously, not to presume. She was Tommy's second wife, a shy, flat-voiced woman. 'You in the dumps too?'

'No,' Fran said. 'Not really.'

In fact, she added to herself, not at all. I'm holding myself still, that's all, so that it won't happen too quickly. So that I won't go spinning too fast into whatever it is that may be – just may be, beginning.

She let these thoughts sweep over her to the point where, suddenly ashamed of her self-absorption, she drew back. 'What about you, El?' she asked. 'Why are you in the dumps?'

'Oh, I dunno. Things. You know. It gets yer down.'

Fran looked at her, smiled weakly, and really did want to know, but Ellie of course would not tell. Not just out of pride, but because she did not believe that Fran, even if her interest was genuine and not just the usual politeness, would understand.

I would, Fran wanted to say. Honestly, I would. Try me! But Ellie only smiled back and looked away.

Fran knew Ellie from the days before Audley's retirement, when, from the Camp, which was less than a mile away, she had kept an eye on the house and a key for visitors. Sitting beside her now, Fran felt a weight of darkness descend that for once had nothing to do with herself.

Occasionally, driving out to collect the keys, she had had a cup of tea in Ellie's kitchen, had sat at the rickety table telling herself, in a self-conscious way: I'm having a cup of tea in the house of a black person.

What she felt now, with a kind of queasiness, was how slight and self-dramatizing her own turmoils were, how she exaggerated all her feelings, took offence, got angry, wept too easily, and all about what?

'See you, El,' she said, very lightly touching the woman's hand. She pushed through to where Angie stood.

'Listen,' she said, 'can we get out of here? I'm being pursued.'

Angie looked interested. 'Who by?'

'You know who,' she said. 'He's got that look. He keeps – hovering.' She frowned. This was only half the truth.

Angie laughed. 'Come on,' she said. 'Let's go down to the beach.'

WHEN Audley returned to the deck, a moment later, Fran was nowhere to be found. He was disappointed. There were things he wanted to ask – things he wanted to say to her.

He set the glass of wine on the rails, an offering, and sat on a chair beside it.

He would have liked to consult her about one or two things. About Clem. About his own life. About Death: would she know anything about that? About love as well, carnal love. Which he thought sometimes he had failed to experience or understand.

Absent-mindedly, he took the glass he had brought for her – forbidden, of course – and sipped, then sipped again. Just as well, he thought, that Madge wasn't around!

VI

FROM the headland above, the sea was flat moonlight all the way to the horizon, but down in the cove among the rocks, almost below sea-level, it rose up white out of the close dark, heaped itself in the narrow opening, then came at them with a rush. Fran leapt back at first, up the shelving sand. 'I don't want to get wet!' She had to yell against the sea as well as get out of the way of it. But when she saw how Angie just let the light wash in around her ankles, then higher, darkening all the lower part of her skirt, she laughed and gave in, but did tuck her dress up. It was grey silk and came to her calves. She did not want it spoiled.

They walked together, Angie half a head taller, along the wet beach, their heels leaving phosphorescent prints, and laughed, talked, regaled one another with stories.

It was a secret place down here. With the sea on one side and the cliffs on the other, you were walled in, but the clouds were so high tonight and the air so good in your lungs that you didn't feel its narrowness, only a deep privacy.

'Do you know this Cedric What's-his-name?' Fran asked after a time. 'Pohl – Cedric Pohl. Isn't that a hoot?'

She disguised the spurt of excitement, of danger she felt at saying the name twice over. 'He's a good-looking boy, isn't he?'

'He isn't a boy,' Angie said. 'He's thirty-three.'

'He asked if he could drive back with me.'

'I thought you were staying.'

'No. That was a mistake. I can't stay.'

They walked on in silence.

'Actually,' Angie said at last, 'he's a bit of a shit.'

'Who is?'

'Your Cedric Pohl.'

'He isn't mine,' Fran said, but it exhilarated her to be speaking of him in these terms.

'So,' she said when a decent interval had elapsed, 'what do you know about him? He's married, I suppose.'

'Was.'

'Well, that's nothing against him.'

'She left him and took the kids. He was two-timing her.'

Fran gave a little laugh, then thought better of it. 'Well,' she said, 'I haven't committed myself. He can go back with the Bergs.'

They came round the edge of the knoll and once again the sea was before them.

A slope, low dunes held together by pigface and spiky grass, led down to the beach. On any other occasion they would have hauled up their skirts at this point and sprinted, but the beach was already occupied. There was a party down there round a leaping fire. They made a face at one another, lifted their skirts like little girls preparing to pee in the open (was that what gave the moment an air of the deliciously forbidden and set them giggling?) and sat plump down in the cool sand to spy.

The fire had been built in the most prodigal way, a great unsteady pyramid of flames. A man with a sleeping bag round his shoulders was tending it, occasionally tossing on a branch but otherwise simply contemplating it, watching the sparks fly up and the nest of heat at its centre breathe and glow. Something in his actions suggested a trancelike meditation, as if the fire had drawn his mind out of him and he were living now as the fire did, subdued to its being but also feeding his and the fire's needs. Watching him you too felt subdued yet invigorated, taken out of yourself into its overwhelming presence.

They sat with their arms round their knees, unspeaking, and the silence between them deepened. Drawn in by the slow gestures of the man as he tossed branch after branch on to the pyre – and, like him, by the pulse of the fire itself, which was responding in waves to the breeze that came in from the sea, and which they felt on the hairs of their arms – they might have stepped out of time entirely.

The others – there were three little groups of them – lay away from the fire but still in the light of its glow.

One couple was curled spoon-fashion on the sand. In the curve of the woman's body, a child, its plump limbs rosy with firelight.

A little distance away another woman sat on a pile of blankets with a baby at her breast and a boy of six or seven beside her. He had his thumb in his mouth.

Further off, where the darkness began, two men sat cross-legged and facing one another so that their brows almost touched.

One, his long hair over his eyes, his head bent, was playing a mouth-organ, some Country and Western tune, very sad and whining, to which the second man beat a rhythm on his thigh.

All around them, scattered without thought in the sand, were bottles, paper plates, cartons, the remains of their meal.

The group of the man, woman and baby shifted a little. The man's arm had gone numb. He eased it, and the woman's body moved with his into a new position. She drew the baby in.

The man with the sleeping bag threw another branch on to the fire.

I could sit here for ever, Fran thought. If the fire went on burning and the man fed it and the others slept like that, and those two men kept on playing that same bit of a tune, I could sit here till I understood at last what it all means: why the sea, why the stars, why this lump in my throat.

Still seated in the sand with her skirt tucked between her knees and her spine straight, she saw herself get up and walk slowly to where the man with the sleeping bag stood. He turned, and without surprise, watched her come in out of the dark. She stood before him for a moment, then, as if granted permission, went and lay down on the sand among the others, between the group of the man, woman and baby and the woman with the small boy, feeling the fire's warmth on one side and the breath of the sea on the other. The tune went on. She slept. And in her dream saw a thin, tight-lipped woman with big eyes like a bush-baby's, sitting far off in the dark of the dunes. Gently she beckoned to her, and the woman got up and came into the circle of light.

Long minutes had passed. They had grown cold. Angie wrapped her arms around herself and shivered. She got to her feet and began to walk on. Fran took up her shoes and followed.

The track led to the crest of the hill. From there a second track would take them down to the horse-paddocks, then the long way round to the house. But as they climbed there was a brighter glow in the sky.

'What is it?' Fran asked. 'More bonfires?'

Then they came to the top and saw it. Great shoots of flame over the town.

VII

FROM the house a fleet of cars had already set off, their progress slowed by the many gates that had to be opened. They were barely out of sight when the telephone rang.

'Poor Audley,' Madge said when Milly Gates from the Post Office gave her the news. She sat down in her black frock, closed her eyes and, worn out with all the preparations and the talk and because it was the only way she had of dealing with things, immediately fell asleep, her head back, snoring.

The half-dozen guests who had stayed behind with her were embarrassed, but felt free now to step out on to the deck and watch from a distance the play of flames across the inlet and the reflected glow in the sky.

In the cars they were still in doubt, as they came along the edge of the Lake, what it was that was making such a show.

'Looks like the police station,' Rupe ventured.

'No,' Ralph told him gloomily, having a good idea what it must be, 'it's not the cop shop.'

Tommy Molloy, sitting in the back seat between them, said nothing. He knew what it was. So did Audley. A vision of it had appeared spontaneously in Audley's head, the four rooms and all their objects in glowing outline, in a red essence of themselves, a final intensity of their being in the world before they collapsed into ash.

He sat very still in the front seat beside Jonathon, wearing a look, behind the startled eyes, of practised stoicism.

The first one away had been Barney Shannon in his ute, with Lily in the cabin beside him. When they came to the gates it was Barney who leapt out and ran forward in the headlamps' beam to open them.

In procession they crossed the causeway into town.

The street was jammed with cars. On the roofs of some of them young fellows in boardshorts were standing as if at a football match, with beer cans in their fists. Girls were being hauled up beside them, slipping and shrieking. Further on was the inner circle of those who had pushed in as close as the heat would allow.

Abandoning the cars, they began to ease their way through the crowd, Ralph staying as close as he could to his father's side. People turned to protest, but, when they saw who it was, made way, and Audley, finding himself the object of so much attention, felt his heart flutter.

A young fireman came hurrying up. He was in uniform but without his helmet.

'Sorry about this, Mr Tyler,' he shouted, 'she's pretty far gone. Old stuff. That's what done it. Went up like a haystack.'

He was a fresh-faced fellow of twenty-two or -three, recently married. The firebell must have got him out of bed. His hair was wild, his face aglow. There was something hectic and unreliable in his looks. He shouted as if afraid his rather high voice might not carry across the distance he felt between himself and a world that was entirely occupied now by the blaze; all the time casting quick little glances over his shoulder, anxious that if he took his eyes off it for even a second, this conflagration, this star-blaze whose heat he felt between his shoulder blades, and which sent runnels of sweat down his sides under the heavy uniform, might die on him before he had time to savour the excitement it had set off in him. Suddenly, unable to resist any longer the attraction of the thing, he swung round and took the full blast of it on his cheeks. He had, Audley saw, a proprietorial look.

Beautiful! His look said. She's a real beauty! It was his first big do.

If I were a policeman, thought Audley, I'd arrest that boy on the spot.

Surprised by his own excitement, which he had caught from the young fireman and which he felt too in the silent concentration and glow of the crowd, he approached the flames.

Don Wheelwright, the local policeman, materialized. 'Don't worry, Mr Tyler,' he shouted, 'we'll get 'em soon enough, the bastards that done it.'

Audley did not respond. He knew who the fellow was referring to. And Don Wheelwright, feeling snubbed, put another mark in his book of grievances. He had had go-ins with Audley before. His promise of action was a challenge. Well, what about it, Mr Tyler? Now it's something of yours the bastards have touched. As if, Audley thought, in Clem, he had not been touched already.

All these unofficial reports were an embarrassment to him, he did not want them. He had no doubt Don Wheelwright and his people would come up with a culprit – several, perhaps. There might even be among them the one who had struck the match. But standing here in the crowd was like being in the fire itself, there was such an affinity between the two, such a surge of intensity. It stilled the mind, sucked up attention and subdued the individual spirit in such a general heightening of crowd-spirit, of primitive joy in the play of wind and flame, that he found himself saying, with grim humour, out of the centre of it: 'So we got our bonfire after all – want it or not.'

He felt, against all sense or reason, exhilarated, released. He could have shaken his palms in the air and danced.

Looking about quickly to see if anyone, Lily for instance, had noticed, he was struck again by the intensity of the faces. They were like sleepwalkers who had come out, some of them still in their nightwear, to gaze on something deeply dreamed.

What we dare not do ourselves, he found himself thinking, they do for us, the housebreakers, the muggers, the smashers, the grab merchants. When we punish them it is to hide our secret guilt. There is ancient and irreconcilable argument in us between settlement and the spirit of the nomad, between the makers of order and our need to give ourselves over at moments to the imps and demons, to the dervish dance of what is in the last resort dust. We are in love with what we most fear and hide from, death. And there came into his head some lines of a poem he had read, composed of course by one of the unsettled:

And yet, there is only
one great thing,
the only thing:
to live to see, in huts and on journeys,
the great day that dawns,
the light that fills the world.

As for the objects in there, brilliantly alive for a moment in the last of what had been their structure and about to fall into themselves as ash – the dining table with its set and empty places, each occupied now by an eddy of flame, the writhings on the double bed, the glass cases exploding and tossing their rocks back into the furnace of time – what was that but a final sacrifice, like his bones, to the future and its angels, whose vivid faces are turned towards us but with sealed lips?

He glanced sideways, feeling an eye upon him.

It was Lily. Tilted at a precarious angle on her stick, her silks all flame, her twist of a smile saying: Don't think I can't see right through you, Audley Tyler, you sorrowful old hypocrite.

He too must have been smiling. She pitched a little and, using her stick to right herself, dipped her shoulder in acknowledgment and turned away.

There is no hope, he told himself, that's what the old know, that's our secret. It is also our hope, our salvation.

It was then that he remembered Tommy. Searching among the nearby crowd, he found him standing a little way off to the left, his face gleaming with sweat. He was watching along with the rest, and as always seeing the thing, the fire in this case, out of another history.

Audley, touched, went across and laid a hand on his old friend's shoulder. They had been through so much together, he and this old man, over the years. Battles won and lost; the night, which might so easily have divided them, of Clem's accident. They looked at one another, but only briefly, then stood side by side without speaking and went on gazing into the fire.

VIII

'Listen,' Clem said, 'listen, everybody. I want to say something.'

They were a small group now, seated on the coarse-bladed lawn with just the lights from the house falling on them through the open windows, only one or two among them, Audley, Lily, in deck chairs; Barney Shannon lay full-length with his hands folded on his chest, but not sleeping. Subdued, each one, by the recent event, which no one referred to, but also by the overwhelming presence, at this hour, now that the music had packed up and they had run out of talk, of the moon, running full-tilt against a bank of fast-moving clouds, and by the bush, so dense and alive with sound, and down in the cove, the sea breaking. Clem could not have said which of these things moved him most. They were all connected.

The day was over, past, if what you meant by that was time strictly measured – it was past midnight. But what he meant by it was the occasion, though that too might end if one of them now made the move, got up and said: 'Well, I'm off,' or 'Let's call it a day,' or 'Me for the blanket show.' The group would break up then, and these last ones, the survivors, would go to join those who were already curled up in bunks and sleeping-bags on their way to the next thing. Tomorrow. He wanted to forestall that. Something more was needed. Something had to be said. And if no one else was ready to say it, then it was up to him. He felt their eyes upon him, and saw Audley's look of disquiet and shook his head, meaning to reassure him: Don't worry, Dad, I know what I'm doing. It's all right.

He felt confident. The words were there, he still had hold of them. And these were friends, people he loved, who would understand if what he said went astray and did not come out the way he meant. Their faces, which just a moment ago had seemed weary and at an end, were expectant. A light of alertness and curiosity was in them, a rekindling.

'Listen,' he said, 'this is what I want to say.

'Out there – out there in space, I mean – there's a kind of receiver. Very precise it is, very subtle – refined. What it picks up, it's made that way, is heartbeats, just that. Every heartbeat on the planet, it doesn't miss a single one, not one is missed. Even the faintest, it picks it up. Even some old person left behind on the track, too weak to go on, just at their last breath. Even a baby in its humidicrib.' He took a breath, growing excited now. He had to control the spit in his mouth as well as the sentences. But he had their attention, it did not matter that one or two of them were frowning and might wonder if he was all there.

'Once upon a time, all this bit of the planet, all this – land mass, this continent – was silent, there was no sound at all, you wouldn't have known it was here. Silence. Then suddenly a blip, a few little signs of life. Not many. Insects, maybe, then frogs, but it was registering their presence. The receiver was turned towards it and tuned in and picked them up. Just those few heartbeats. What a weak little sound it must have been, compared with India for instance or China, or Belgium even – that's the most crowded spot. How could anyone know how big it was with so few heartbeats scattered across it? But slowly others started to arrive, just a few at first, rough ones, rough – hearts – then a rush, till now there are millions. Us, I mean, the ones who are here tonight. Now. There's a great wave of sound moving out towards it, a single hum, and the receiver can pick up each one, each individual beat in it, this one, that one – that's how it's been constructed, that's what it's fixed to do. Only it takes such a long time for the sound to travel across all that space that the receiver doesn't even know as yet that we've arrived – us whites, I mean. Our heartbeats haven't even got there yet. But that doesn't matter—' he laughed, it was going well '—because we *are* here, aren't we? Others were here, now they're gone. But their heartbeats are still travelling out. Even though they stopped ages ago, they're still travelling. It doesn't matter one way or the other, which people, the living or the dead, it's all the same. Or whether they're gone now or still here like us. The birds too. You can feel the way their hearts beat when you pick one up, even when it's still in the shell. And rabbits. What I think is—' he prepared now for his conclusion '—is this. If we imagined ourselves out there and concentrated hard enough, really concentrated, we could hear it too, all of it, the whole sound coming towards us, all of it. It's possible. Anything is possible. Nothing is lost. Nothing ever gets *lost*.'

He looked about, their attention was on him. And suddenly there was nothing more to say.

'That's all,' he said abruptly, 'that's all I wanted to say. Because of what day it is. You know, because of that. Because no one had said anything. So I did.'

He smiled nervously but felt pleased with himself. He felt good about things. He grinned, gave a little laugh, then sat on the grass and saw that they were all smiling, except for Audley, who always had a few tears on these occasions. But that was all right. It was good. Only he wished that Fran had still been here. She had left half an hour ago and that put a dampener on his heart, but not so much of a one. That was all right too. They could go to bed now. He could. They all could. The day was over.

But not yet, not quite yet. They would sit for a bit, letting the moon, the dark surrounding bush with its medley of night-sounds, hold them in its single mood, which his speech had not broken.

Fran had left in a group of a dozen or so, including Cedric Pohl, who did go with the Bergs. The cars made a procession down the rutted slope and through the three gates to the main road.

In the flurry of farewells, in the leaping torchlight as people stumbled over clods and picked their way among bushes to find their cars, she had had no chance to explain to Clem, simply to say what he already understood, that she felt out of things and would rather drive back tonight than in the heat of the day. He nodded, smiling. She kissed him quickly and climbed into her car.

The procession got under way and she closed her mind to everything but the drive ahead: her mind, not her body. The excitement she felt at the prospect of something new, a romance even, had settled now to a slow but regular ticking in her. Like a bomb, she thought, that was timed to explode somewhere up ahead. Well, she'd deal with that when she came to it.

As they swung down past the horse-paddocks and began to climb the moonslope, two figures appeared in the light of the headlamps and had to move away to the side of the road.

It was Ralph and Angie out walking – bailed up now by the line of cars. She would have stopped and spoken, but there were two more cars behind her and before she could wave even, they had been left standing, looking blanched and ghostlike, stunned by the blaze of lights. Still, the image of them together, isolated in the dark, Ralph in his white shirt, Angie in black, pleased her.

Ralph and Angie walked, as they often did at the end of the day, even at home in the city. Sharing a half-hour together after so many in which they had gone their separate ways.

Down here in the open they walked in whatever light there was from the moon, since they knew this place like the back of their hands. At home it was under humming streetlights, past fences behind which dogs leapt or growled and walls scribbled with graffiti – Yuppies Fuck Off or Eve Was Framed – stepping over rubbish spilled out of doorways, old-fashioned hearts drawn in chalk on the pavement and roughly initialled, through streets where the inhabitants were already sleeping; pausing sometimes before a lighted window to catch a couple of moments from a late-night movie. Ralph, who knew every movie ever made, would identify it for her. 'That's Jack Palance, the rat! In *Panic in the Streets*.' Or, 'That's Marilyn in *Bus Stop*.'

They seldom talked, or if they did it was to pass on bits and pieces of the day's news, none of it important. It was the walking together that held them close. Now, as they came up the hill in the dark, they could hear Audley at the piano. He liked to play quietly to himself when the rest of the household had gone to bed:

simple things that he had learned when he was a boy. Tonight it was 'Jesu, Joy of Man's Desiring'. The flowing accompaniment brought them right up to the kitchen steps and they stood a moment in the dark to let him finish.

The piano was an old Bechstein upright, its black enamel finish chipped in places, worn in others. He played without music but with his eyes fixed ahead, as if the pages stood open on their rest; very straight on the stool, still hearing in his head that first voice telling him: Keep your shoulders back, Aud, sit up straight, and don't drop your wrists. Being stern with himself, as he was in everything.

When he came to a conclusion he sat with his hands on his knees, till Ralph called: 'That was great, Dad. We just dropped in to say good night.'

Angie had gone to the tap over the sink to get a glass of water. Nothing had been cleared. In the sink, still in its wrapping, was a big bunch of flowers – tuberoses, the air was drenched with their scent – and under them, Audley's blackfish.

'You go on,' she told Ralph quietly. 'I'll just clear up a bit.'

Ralph kissed her on the back of the neck while she stood and sipped her glass of water, then went to say goodnight to his father. She unwrapped the flowers, found a pail to put them in and ran cold water over the fish to freshen them up, then made room for them in the bottom of the fridge. When she looked up Ralph was gone and Audley was standing in the doorway behind her.

She turned and ran the tap to rinse her hands.

'Would you like me to make some tea?' she asked.

They were the night owls of the household. They often found themselves alone like this, last thing.

He did not like to go to bed, she knew that. He was scared, she suspected, that if he took his clothes off and lay down to sleep he would slip so far into the dark, into the night that becomes greater night, that he might never get back. He had never said any of this, he was too proud, but she had seen the same thing, the year before he died, in her father. Without waiting for an answer now she filled the electric jug and he sat down like a patient child on one of the forms.

The throbbing of the jug filled the silence. When it stopped she was aware, as she had not been before, of the odd little sounds that came from the house itself, its joists and uprights creaking as they shifted and settled like sleepers — or it was the sleepers themselves in their several rooms and out on the deck where the young were sleeping. She thought she could hear Ned, who was inclined to mutter in his sleep.

Taking her cup, she stepped to the window and looked down on half a dozen forms all huddled in their sleeping-bags, and made out Ned's fair head, then Jenny's darker one. All safe as houses.

She came back and sat by Audley at the bench.

'What I've always admired about you, Angie,' he said after a moment, 'is the gift you have for attending — for attention. People never mention it among the virtues, but it might be the greatest of them all. It's the beginning of everything. Malebranche, you know, called it the natural prayer of the soul. I think it's what Clem's speech meant to say. You didn't hear it, did you?'

She shook her head, took a sip from her cup.

'I wish you had. It would have meant something to you. I was deeply moved. By the boy's intense — happiness. He spoke from a full heart — I think he was trying to say something to *me*. You know, about the fire — as well as all the rest. What a day we've had!' He sipped his tea. 'Thank you,' he said in his formal way.

They sat a little longer, saying nothing now.

Outside, a breeze had sprung up; it stirred the faded chintz at the windows, touched with freshness the stale air of the room. On the edge of town, the charred ashes of the museum glowed a moment so that here and there a flame appeared and wetly hissed.

Down in the cove, the bonfire, which had collapsed on itself, a shimmering mass, revived, threw up flames that cast a flickering redness over the sand, and one of the men, conscious perhaps of the renewed heat, sat up for a moment out of sleep and regarded it, then burrowed back into the dark. Till here, as on other beaches, in coves all round the continent, round the vast outline of it, the heat struck of a new day coming, the light that fills the world.

CHILD'S PLAY

In a sunlit piazza on an April morning, women throw buckets of water over the cobbles and men deliver trays of pastry to trattorie. In a barren room above, a fanatic watches, engaged in the details of his life's most important project: the assassination of one of Italy's most beloved men of letters. In this penetrating novella, David Malouf plumbs the darker uses of our passions. Weaving a dense tapestry of psychological observation and personal events of mythic importance, he re-creates the frighteningly fascinating mind of a madman poised at his moment of truth.

Fiction/Literature/0-375-70141-9

THE CONVERSATIONS AT CURLOW CREEK

It is 1827, and in a remote hut high on the plains of New South Wales, two strangers spend the night in talk. One is an illiterate Irishman, an ex-convict and bushranger, who is to be hanged at dawn. The other is the police officer who has been sent to supervise the execution. As the night wears on, the two men share memories and uncover unexpected connections between their lives. Intensely evocative and keenly moving, *The Conversations at Curlow Creek* is a masterpiece.

Fiction/Literature/0-679-77905-1

FLY AWAY PETER

When Ashley Crowther returns to Australia to manage his father's property, he meets Jim Saddler, the young woodsman who becomes Ashley's guide to his inheritance, and the two form an unlikely but durable bond. But when war breaks out in Europe, Jim and Ashley are drawn into the obscene enterprise of the trenches, where death falls from the sky and burrows out of the earth. Combining overwhelmingly sensual imagery with an unblinking consciousness of the worst that history can inflict, *Fly Away Peter* is a novel of phosphorescent beauty and imagination.

Fiction/Literature/0-679-77670-2

The Great World is a remarkable novel of self-knowledge and the fall from innocence. It focuses on the unlikely friendship of two men who meet as POWs of the Japanese during World War II: Digger Keen, strong yet gentle, ruminative, unambitious, and Vic Curran, an orphan from a poor mining community, a tortured, self-made entrepreneur. For both men, war was supposed to be a testing ground of masculine and nationalist virtue. Instead, it becomes an ordeal that lays bare the painful reality which lies behind a nation's myth of itself.

Fiction/Literature/0-679-74836-9

HARLAND'S HALF ACRE

Frank Harland's mother dies from the prick of a rose thorn; his irresponsible father gives him up and then takes him back to help raise the younger children. Yet Frank grows up to be a dreamer, who feels helpless except when he is putting lines on paper and whose attempts to rescue his remaining kinfolk bear tragic consequences. In exploring the enigma of Frank Harland, David Malouf creates a haunting portrait of an Australian artist who is a genuine visionary and a flawed savior to his disintegrating family. *Harland's Half Acre* tells of abandonment and desperate love, of aboriginal landscapes and haunted car parks, of families that refuse to stay together and others that cling until they strangle.

Fiction/Literature/0-679-77647-8

AN IMAGINARY LIFE

In the first century A.D., Publius Ovidius Naso, the most urbane and irreverent poet of imperial Rome, was banished to a remote village on the edge of the Black Sea. From these sparse facts, David Malouf has fashioned an audacious and supremely moving work of fiction. Malouf reimagines Ovid's life in exile, as the poet depends on the kindness of barbarians who impale their dead and converse with the spirit world. And later he becomes the guardian of a feral child who has grown up among deer. Written with dazzlingly lyrical prose, *An Imaginary Life* is a luminous encounter between civilization and nature.

Fiction/Literature/0-679-76793-2

In the mid-1840s, a thirteen-year-old British cabin boy, Gemmy Fairley, is cast ashore in the far north of Australia and taken in by aborigines. Sixteen years later he moves back into the world of Europeans, among hopeful yet terrified settlers who are staking out their small patch of home in an alien place. To them, Gemmy stands as a different kind of challenge: he is a force that at once fascinates and repels. *Remembering Babylon* follows the boy as he struggles to find his identity in a new world.

Short-listed for The Booker Prize
Fiction/Literature/0-679-74951-9

VINTAGE INTERNATIONAL
Available at your local bookstore, or call toll-free to order:
1-800-793-2665 (credit cards only).